A FINE ROMANCE

& OTHER STORIES

Books by John Allman

Poetry

Walking Four Ways in the Wind (Princeton Series of
    Contemporary Poets, 1979)
Clio's Children (New Directions, 1985)
Scenarios for a Mixed Landscape (New Directions, 1986)
Curve Away from Stillness: Science Poems (New Directions,
    1989)
Inhabited World: New & Selected Poems (The Wallace
    Stevens Society Press, 1995)
Loew's Triboro (New Directions, 2004)
Attractions: a chapbook of prose poems (2River Press,
    2006)
Lowcountry (New Directions, 2007)
Older Than Our Fathers: a chapbook (Mudlark, 2008)
Little Songs: a chapbook (Mudlark, 2012)
Algorithms (Quale Press, 2012)

Fiction
Descending Fire & Other Stories (New Directions, 1994)

A FINE
ROMANCE
& OTHER STORIES

JOHN ALLMAN

QUALE PRESS

Grateful acknowledgment is made to the following journals in
which these stories first appeared:
    Ambusharts, "His Story"
    Blackbird, "A Fine Romance," "Dear Sis..." & "Get Up"
    Hotel Amerika, "Godardesque"
    Michigan Quarterly Review, "Waiting for Z"
    Storyglossia, "Darlene Descending"

Cover: General View of North Side of Bridge from New Jersey
Side of River — George Washington Bridge, Spanning Hudson
River between Manhattan & Fort Lee, NJ, New York County,
NY, Library of Congress, Prints & Photographs Division,
HAER, Reproduction number HAER NY,31-NEYO,161—15

ISBN: 978-1-935835-18-9
LCCN: 2016944447

Quale Press
www.quale.com

CONTENTS

for Dan Masterson,
his inspiring poems,
his keen eye,
his enduring friendship

A FINE ROMANCE

DURING A HUMID, *windless afternoon on the island of St. John, Tiffany Longworth, duped by a counterfeit taxi driver just after she left the boat from St. Thomas, was being ~~dragged~~ whisked ~~carted~~ to a small hotel in Cinnamon Bay. And though the kidnappers seemed in disagreement whether to ask for money or the release of political prisoners, there was no doubt that Corso was the leader — his white teeth, dark visage and courtly voice almost reminding her of the ~~husband~~ lover she'd only two weeks ago broken up with. She kept finding something attractive in him, as if her will to believe that would undo the reality of what was happening in this hotel room, where the electric fan mounted on the wall blew a ~~febrile, halitotic[?], dying, feeble~~ fetid breath so like exhaustion that Tiffany realized just how fatigued she herself was.*

Now two of Corso's men were trying to assure her that she wouldn't be hurt — the short one with the Indian profile ~~picking~~ sucking his teeth. She was terribly hungry, aware of a dull fear that the stuffy hotel room would be home for a long time, while the still air outside buzzing with mosquitoes was a worse alternative, the ~~phony~~ entire brochure-image of her visit to St. John becoming stained with the ~~sordid~~ poverty and want of these ~~primitive~~ unhappy men. Her only hope was to get a message to the American sailors who were carousing next door. Or to draw Corso closer, to convince him that her family would not put up a ransom. That she had a disease...

"Ugh!"

The phone ~~throbbed insistently~~ rang. Trudy Devereux, wearing a T-shirt that depicted a map of several Caribbean islands sprawling downward over her unbound breasts, had already filled almost twelve long yellow pages and flipped them over the back of the pad. Reluctantly, she pushed the "Talk" button. She knew it would be Ray, her ex. She hoped it would be Frederick, her new lover — the conductor, his plump hand waving the baton that made so many instruments work in unison.

"What?" she said.

"You must be writing," Ray said.

"And?"

"I want you to see what I'm working on."

She imagined him in his loft, paintings leaning against a wall, his long hair beginning to gray, some woman's underwear tossed on a chair, his smile like a forgery of the Mona Lisa's. They liked each other better as friends and sometime lovers, so they had separated, but she'd kept him on her Authors Guild health insurance until the divorce.

She huffed. "Why is it always a bad time for me but a good one for you?"

"No, no, no. Not *now*. I really want you to see this. How about one thirty? Then lunch?"

"Can you keep your hands to yourself?"

"Promise! I'm sorry I interrupted you. You know I love your work."

"You used to!" She ~~flicked fucked~~ clicked him off.

In the current annual romance writing conventions held in places like New Orleans, he might have been one of the long-haired models in leather jock-straps, hooted at and cheered by a crowd of women; the men like Lacedaemonian warriors preening before a battle with the Persian Army, only here the prize of battle was a modeling contract and appearance on the cover of a romance novel. He'd appeared on the cover of Trudy's first book years ago, just for income, he'd said, since his art was not selling anywhere. Following her time with Ray she could write for days, sometimes in a kind of softened twilight state, and she became not only her heroine but the men who appeared out of dark corners, the men in Italian suits who boarded planes and wore rings with mysterious crests, the men with creased smiles and resonant voices who would be cruel in bed and later arrange for flowers to be brought with breakfast. But ever since 9/11 she'd been asking herself if she wanted to write this kind of book when people were being blown to bits only as far away as the nearest radio or TV, though the idea of *relevance* made her sick. Her field was so crowded! All those younger readers, all those subscribers to the *Romance Writers Report*, submitting their novels to contests like "The Golden Heart," "Love and Laughter," "The Winning Man," "From the Heart," scanning the reports for the latest interests of Avon Romance or Ballantine Books or Harlequin Mills & Boon, Ltd. or Leisure Books or Silhouette Books (who were getting out of the Paranormal category but were interested in twists on twins that change places, or books that contained a kidnapping — which she was doing!).

And if the sailors next door came to her rescue? Would they rape her in the heat of that moment? Would she now be able to seize the revolver one of the men had rested on the teak bureau? Corso's voice caressing the air. The danger of this moment intertwined with the boredom that had driven her to come here in the first place. She looked at Corso, at the revolver that looked dusty and unused, at the men who twitched to his commands, his authority filling the room with vibrant energy.

She was going to Frederick's rehearsal of his orchestra in Ossining tonight. She didn't have time for Ray this afternoon and ought to have said so. Frederick. *Fred.* Last week he'd taken her to a Middle-Eastern restaurant in Nyack. The old brick structure housing the restaurant had once been the town jail, and in the rear, on the way to the rest room, she passed a barred window in an original wall. On the other side of it was a small room, one of the old cells, and a table covered with flowers. A plaque commemorated the jail, which had been built at the turn of last century. She imagined a bunk bed, a prisoner who smoked too much, a toilet bowl without seat, a rust-stained sink. Overhead these days he'd have a small TV that blared until curfew. Somewhere there must be a surveillance camera. Being observed day and night in itself a punishment. Maybe Corso had been treated this way. Maybe this is how he'd gathered his little gang, meeting with them after their joint release, filled with resentment against the gringo world.

Later, as the boat pulled away from the island, she felt the wind in her face, the spray that needled its coldness up and down her legs in her ~~orange~~ white slacks (thank God she'd taken more than shorts and the ~~adorable~~ flimsy Donna Karan top).

"Señorita, you wish to smoke?" One of the men, short, square, offered her a cigarette from his crumpled pack. He smelled of unwashed clothes. Work. Anxiety. Manured fields. Kitchens with no ventilation. Fried plantain. Urine.

"No, no!"

That dinner in Nyack, she had worn long white pants and a blue, sleeveless top, its first three buttons undone, abundant freckles sprinkled like confetti along her arms and across her modest cleavage. Too much sun, she knew, but she couldn't help it. Before they sat down, she'd bent over the table to scoop up white dip with a spear of raw carrot, and she knew that Frederick was admiring the tightness of her rear end, her straight, narrow legs, the small, exploratory bites she took of her crudité. Attractive, too, were the taut lines of her face — the dramatic slope of her cheekbones partly the result of sunken tissue around the upper lip, as she began to age. But she was beautiful. She had the look of models who had had their rear molars extracted. Her eyes shone. Frederick ran his hand up and down her back, sliding it over her bare shoulder, down her arm.

"Deje de hacer eso! Vayese! You!" *Leaning out of the pilot cabin, Corso waved the man away from her. Then he said something that Tiffany understood to mean they would split up in Charlotte Amalie. But she couldn't make out who she'd be with. She was hungry and she was settling into ~~a debilitating ennui~~ boredom. The coolness of the ~~twilight wavering green indifferent~~ crepuscular sea failed to invigorate either her earlier terror or her reason. Perhaps, she thought, she was fatigued and was losing too much sense of how desperate her situation was. She looked up at Corso who had stepped out of the cabin and was facing the ever-nearer Charlotte Amalie, its lights and tilting boats, his profile like something she remembered from an old ~~dream magazine and her mother's album~~ movie. The image of the woman, the actress, in that film, whatever it was, had almost formed in her mind, when two of her captors began singing, holding their arms outward to embrace the ~~sun heated acrid saline~~ sea-spray air, their small dark heads like those of Guatemalan clay figures she'd seen in an exhibit in the American Museum of Natural History. They sang on key, with little yipping sounds and laughter.*

In the dining area, there had been two men with balalaikas, and one man with a drum between his legs. She was thumping her foot to the music, her forehead gleaming like porcelain, her small ears like perfect sculptures, but she refused Frederick's invitation to dance. Frederick, stout and perspiring, at times scholarly looking in the way he pursed his lips, was aglow from the wine and the beat of the instruments. His boyish demeanor was the sort seen in medieval paintings of saints, in contrast to the testy patron who had commissioned the work and was lurking in the shadows — something Frederick knew from a father who had been for so long critical of his son's attempts at a career. "You should work with me," he'd said, "where the real world is." But real estate and insurance simply did not galvanize Frederick the way Brahms or Mozart did, especially when he was up at the podium with his baton, controlling the harmonies of all those instruments, all that exuberance — all those men and women in their chairs, reading the sheet music before them, looking up for his guidance, their hands invisibly tethered to his will. Somewhere in the midst of all his plumpness, at times Trudy could see authority, self-knowledge.

And if she ran, Tiffany thought, if she could lose herself among the street people in Charlotte Amalie, Corso would never risk shooting at her. Corso. His name ~~rattled~~ reverberated in her being like a church bell in Venice, echoing among the pensiones and trattorias, dispersing itself in the openness of the Grand Canal. Corso. She imagined sitting with him in

San Marco's, near one of the several orchestras, this one playing Debussy, the thin waiter taking their order for champagne, dusk drifting over the lagoons like fragrant smoke.

The phone rang. "Shit!" She thought it was Ray.

"It's me. Else."

Her friend Else Thompson, whose cabin was opposite her own at Blessing Lake.

"As if I didn't know who 'me' is by now."

"We're a bit cranky this morning." Else played one of the two cellos in Frederick's orchestra and never hesitated to be direct — asking, once she learned Trudy was dating the conductor, "Does he make good music in bed?"

'It's this new book."

"Well, I won't keep you. The Lake Association wants to use chemicals to control the weeds. I'm concerned about the geese. We need to speak up."

Else, a widow and occasional journalist, was good at that, pressing for road repairs on the dirt track that led to the cabins or insisting on rules for playing music at night because of renters who liked to sing in their canoes under a full moon. She enlisted Trudy's help whenever she could.

"What do you want me to do?"

"Write a letter."

"Really, I'm very busy. What do I care about those filthy birds who always deposit their green turds on my lawn?"

"You're such a city girl! This is important!"

"I thought that copper sulfate was safe. Isn't that what they're using?"

"If we had children, we wouldn't feel so safe. Never mind the geese."

Trudy could imagine her gray-haired steely friend slowly beginning to raise a fist. She understood how the woman had escaped the Nazis in her native Norway.

"Just one letter," Else continued.

"Saying?"

They parried back and forth until Trudy agreed and Else asked, "Are you going to rehearsal tonight?"

"If I ever get there!"

When she looked up at Corso, she saw him drawing on the pad on his lap. He was sketching the approaching city, the prow of the boat breasting the sea, and she could feel a pressure within her, as if she too were plowing through salty currents in an aftermath of love. He held up the pad for her to observe his work. The charcoal strokes were bold and rhythmic, capturing the sensation of the ~~orgasmically~~ *rolling boat, and in his fabricated distance was the suggestion of crowded streets. If only she could lose herself there, slip away, disappear somewhere into that scene.*

Trudy pulled off at the Canal Street exit and parked across the street in front of an auto repair shop opposite an old industrial building, where Ray occupied the top floor. The dust from 9/11 that had coated the street, the buildings, the parked cars, the faces of pedestrians, the shop windows, had become a dingy gray that even now seemed to inhabit the air. The floor beneath Ray's studio loft was rented by a Black repertory company that produced original one-act plays. A fire door could be triggered open by any of the tenants from their living quarters. She pushed Ray's bell and looked around the unrehabilitated interior of the ground floor, always on the *qui vive* for details. The scaling plaster of the walls and the ochre-stained ceiling looked like the theater set of a war drama. There were barrels filled with refuse, old lathing, crumpled embossed tin and broken linoleum tiles wrapped in plastic. In the dust left by construction work, she could see the delicate footprints of rats.

Ray buzzed her in.

"Hey! What do you think? Not bad, eh?" Corso held the sketch against his broad chest. Then he leaned forward and whispered, "Don't worry. I will take care of you." For a moment, she believed him. What could be more assuring than to be in his enfolding muscular, hairless, sun-bleached [haired huh?] arms, while the deep blue of a Caribbean evening absorbed the heat rippling up from the beaches and traffic of St. Thomas, cooling the decks of cruise ships, a rich hue pervading her body with excitement, as if the city that was her being had flung open its doors, and the same ineluctable physics lowering the temperature of the busy port had also released a shimmering heat from her ~~turbulent~~... wracked... sensate... ~~animal~~ soul.

She had to shield her eyes from the bright light coming into the loft, which had once been the third floor of a printing plant. On a long work table was the equipment he used for photography and design. He'd built a little dark room against the wall. Lately, he implied he had a big project coming up. Really big, he said, and winked. Two living areas had been walled off, on either side of a huge rectangle, leaving an immense space between what was lit in the daytime primarily by the sun flowing through the safety glass of the skylight. Ray had attached two rows of aluminum reflectors to enhance the light on cloudy days — the way they used to, he said, on the old outdoor sets in Hollywood, in D. W. Griffith's day, which had accounted for the squint of characters in *The Birth of a Nation*.

Tiffany looked up and noted Corso's uplifted profile against the bluish light, as the boat swerved into the harbor, but more impressive were his sketches in the pad that he was allowing her to examine. Some were of another place, a sugar-cane field, with workers in straw hats; there was a mill with smokestacks; and smaller studies with piles of thick stalks, peasants with boots and shotguns. There were trees with zigzags carved in their trunks, and a fine linear outline of a bird like one of the petroglyphs she'd seen in pictures of the old plantation forest on St. John. Corso laughed and she looked up. He said, "Did you know my great grandfather was a Sephardic Jew?" As the boat slowed down and puttered toward its mooring, one of the men began to ~~snort cough inhale a white powder off a~~ *sing, and Corso, looking at her, put his finger to his lips, to warn her not to say or try anything. It was becoming like a tour, she thought. So far, what abuses had she suffered? And who would care? Who would care she had been* ~~slashed across the face~~ *kidnapped?*

The sun, glancing off huge mirrors, was in their eyes. Ray had neglected to fold up his reflectors, which now blazed with light directly over the portable easel on which he had set his enlarged, textured photos, which he had further altered by whiting out the details irrelevant to his purpose.

"I can hardly see anything in this light!" Trudy complained. She had already seen enough. Ray had enlarged the cover of her first book, *Passion in Velvet*, but this version featured a commercial artist's version of Ray himself as the long-haired, shirtless Adonis leaning over a newly awakened adolescent girl. At least, that's what she was now. Originally, she had been a well-endowed blonde, her hair splayed out on a plush maroon pillow, her body twisted to one side in an access of eroticized grief. Ray had thinned the woman's body. Reduced the breasts to nascent curves. Made the V of her crotch narrower, longer. And replaced the fixed stare of need with a look of innocent amazement.

"What is she supposed to be admiring," Trudy asked, "your penis?"

"Well, if the shoe fits!" Ray guffawed.

Against the wall he turned the steel crank that folded the reflectors out of the way and then rushed to join her. His jeans were old and puffy at the knees. The odor of turpentine coming off his hands was not only giving her a headache, but seeping through her mouth into her taste buds — as if she'd been sucking mentholated lozenges. Dotting the outlines of the man and girl in the photo-poster were sequins, and Ray had textured part of their faces with a kind of gray stucco material.

Tiffany noted that one of her captors had coarse, calloused hands. She wondered if he had worked in the cane fields. How his pencil-thin torso could flex and stiffen in love. Why was she thinking such things when her life was in danger? Or was it? The men were so courteous.

But with the reflected light out of her eyes, she could now take in the other photo-poster, or painting, or whatever he called it. It was based on a blow-up of her photo that had appeared on the back cover of *Passion in Velvet*. Evidently, he hadn't dared to encrust her visage with extraneous materials, but the outlines around her eyes were dark as though from excess mascara, and he had somehow lengthened her cheeks to give her a drawn and serious look that resembled the hunger drawn into the faces of vampires. Most of her features had been whited out, her mouth a smudge of black ink, her nose two bullet-hole nostrils, but Ray had succeeded in conveying in this face that was not quite a cartoon, loneliness and pride. Anger. And she hated him for it, for flaunting his own cleverness. At least he hadn't aged her terribly. But he could have! She upbraided herself for being anywhere near him. What did he want? She declined his offer of lunch. Money, he must be needing money, she thought.

"What do you want me to say?' she asked.

"Say if you like it or not. I don't want you to feel insulted." He put his arm around her waist.

She could feel his fingers closing into a grip. Pulling her toward him.

"Well, I'm not. And you can just stop that. I hope you're not broke again."

"Did I say I was?" He held his hands up. "Did I ask you for anything? Jesus!"

"Since you ask, I think they're puerile. Something out of Andy Warhohl's trash can. Whatever do you have in mind?"

"It's satire!" he said. "That's just the point. It's meant to be trash."

"And me? And my book? Are we trash?"

"No, no, no. It's all about *presentation*. How it spins off into a world by itself." He leaned against a nearby work table, hands palms up. "Don't you see?" His pony tail, half-gray, dry, looked disreputable, his hair odorous — not the glistening mane of years ago, not the attractively aged hair that fell loose and framed his face in her bedroom at the cabin as he bent over her, *his joy a moaning counterpoint to the brittle song of crickets*. Was that only last year?

"Well, let me know how it turns out. I'll try to see what you mean. But I don't know if I can." Already, she felt sorry for him, the way his talent bent itself to a commercial hope. She kissed him on the cheek and left, but not before rubbing up against him as she pulled away. Ray smiled unhopefully.

The small boat they were in now allowed the swell from their headlong progress to rush over the sides, for it rode through the water deep in the stern. The Indian-looking men with deep tans scrutinized her from time to time, almost like third-world doctors in a squalid clinic, and she shuddered. Corso was at the wheel in the little pilot cabin, clenching a cigarillo in his teeth (Tiffany thought of a movie with Zachary Scott, his thin, triangular face, the satanic embezzler's smile), smoke creating a haze around his head. He had before him a

*long, wide sketching pad. She longed for a bath. And
as the distance closed between St. John and the port
of Charlotte Amalie, the phosphorus wake of the green
water a glowing hem that trailed behind them, one of the
men spat overboard, making an ugly sound in his throat.
He looked at her defiantly and one more iota of hope
unmoored itself from her thoughts. Could Corso control
them? She hadn't yet focused on the contradiction
forming in her soul, that Corso, the leader of this entire
venture — which had so little shape or meaning to it —
was also her savior.*

Trudy sat in the space of the Eucharistic chapel
at Maryknoll Seminary. She didn't want to be very
much in evidence as Frederick conducted rehearsal.
During the actual performance of the *Magnificat* in
January, there would be a gate or screen and she'd
be able to see only the side of the choral group that
would be divided into two parts facing each other over
the heads of the orchestra and Frederick's pumping
arms. Just now he was leaning over his sheet music,
his hand poised in the air, while the players in the
string section — including Trudy's friend Else and the
widower Leonard Abernathy — stared straight ahead,
their bows upright, wisps of fatigue drifting across
the faces of those who'd come here after a full day's
work. Opposite the musicians, and on their wooden
grandstand, were the singers, not yet in the outfits
they'd wear for the performance, the long skirts,
the open gowns, the men in tuxes or dark suits —
everyone tonight in chinos, skirts, cotton slacks. For

some reason the singers seemed more energized than the orchestra.

Sitting here now, in the recess among the cool marble and the empty tabernacle and the faint hint of rose water, looking at the back of Frederick's somewhat pear-shaped silhouette, the baton firm in his pinched fingers, Trudy thought of Ray as he used to be. A forbidden urge swept over her, as she peered past the rehearsal group down into the enormous space of the basilica, looking up at the high ceiling, its cross beams, dropping her gaze down along the columns, behind which was a vaulted walkway with stained-glass scenes depicting the Stations of the Cross. She almost imagined making love here, Ray holding a blanket over them in the high, draughty sacred space.

The other night at dinner, Frederick had been in a nearly manic state, as he'd rattled on about music and his childhood and his father, the man who had not believed in him. It was almost interesting, to watch her new lover discuss his redemption from a parent's ill will, knowing later he'd be damp from hours of perspiring, his ego wide and hungry in spite of fatigue, something too demanding in his embrace. She knew that somehow she was using Ray to make it more interesting to be with Frederick later, when she would watch his amazement as she undressed and drew him to her and listened to his breathless praise, felt the slow enfolding of his heat around her, the cascading collops of his love, her orgasms an incoming rush of tide, wave after wave, Frederick squealing, she herself dilating into an infantile field of total sensation, almost passing out as Frederick flowed into his condom and her limbs seemed to extend themselves to every corner of the room, her body throbbing...

She thought of Tiffany Longworth trying to escape to St. Thomas. Pursuit down the streets of Charlotte Amalie, among the street hawkers and pimps. But she stopped herself from going further. Instead, while the singers began their harmonies, she thought about the Chinese motifs in the external appearance of Maryknoll, its green-tiled roof high above the Hudson River and the downward slope to Ossining and the prison. Getting to the chapel, she'd passed a series of paintings in which Christ was preaching to Chinese children, in a flat landscape. All one saw of him was his back, his raised arms, his lemony aureole the same hue as the interiors of peonies. Thinking now of Tiffany and Corso and Ray and Frederick seemed no more out of place than these pictures of Christ speaking Aramaic, proselytizing Asian children in the middle of bosky northern Westchester.

Corso spun the wheel and the boat came about. His two underlings stopped singing and grew serious, looking astern at the suddenly receding Charlotte Amalie as Corso steered them back through the remnants of their own wake. They were returning to St. John and Tiffany didn't know why. Corso was ~~patriarchal~~[?] imperious, and when they docked in Cruz Bay, within sight of the regular ferries from St. Thomas and the crowd of taxi drivers harassing the disembarking tourists, he rapidly issued instructions in Spanish to his men who positioned themselves between Tiffany and the side of the boat that was now bumping against the little pier.

"I will be back," he said to her. "Do not worry."

He leaped onto the dock and she couldn't help but admire his adroitness, though for the first time she felt truly afraid. Never before had he left her alone with the other men. And as she observed him swing his ~~narrow-hipped~~ way hurriedly toward the ferry berth, she heard the Indian — it was the only way she could think of him — mutter something to the other man, who was very dark, with a poorly trimmed mustache, eyes bloodshot from drink or the salt spray that had been in their faces as they sped back from Charlotte Amalie. She looked at the men and they smiled — their glistening teeth like an ad, if she could ignore the stained T-shirts and the glandular odors of work that wafted from their ancient seeming bodies like stale sex.

ALL THAT NIGHT and into morning, Trudy dreamt of her first husband, Josh Devereux, and relived the accident that had taken his life. When she woke, she could still see his pianist's hands gripping the wheel. And her father. The dream had also brought him back. Now, in its aftermath, she remembered the evenings he had spent in his study, until he stood up, all six-foot-seven of him, pipe clenched in his teeth, the fiction he churned out receiving the axe by anonymous editors, his aggrieved face harder to re-adjust each morning as he went to his teaching job in Hartford, Connecticut. Her mother had given up an adventurous youth for a man with the kind of modest ambition that, while keeping them away from undue risk, did not carry their income aloft.

The war had something to do with all that. At least so Trudy surmised. She was born after her father had come back from Europe. She knew he'd been among those soldiers who'd opened the death camps. "You really don't want to know," he told her.

She remembered her mother's warnings about gaining weight. What she oughtn't to eat. They would practice at luncheons in the good hotels how to be crisp with headwaiters, how to steer among the creamy desserts, how not to mention the daughter who'd died before Trudy was born. If that lost daughter was the sorrow that dragged at her father, she had to give her mother credit for not pretending there was nothing wrong. Both her parents at times would sit opposite each other in the living-room generating pain so tangible that walking between them was like breast-stroking through the icy early morning waters of a mountain lake. It was simpler if she went into her room and read her Nancy Drew mysteries. Or played with Samantha, the huge Angora cat, who sooner or later raked her arm or leg, behaving only for her mother. Or tried the make-up she'd bought with her friend Angela. Or listened to the Rubinstein recordings her father loved so much. She had theories about her parents. Perhaps the first child was not by her father. Perhaps her mother so detested his literary ambition that she'd ruined the both of them with mockery and resentment. Or Trudy herself was a disappointment, avoiding her parents once she went to Oberlin, not finishing her degree, running away with her piano teacher, a divorced man awakened to sudden conscience by the war beginning in Southeast Asia, but not skilled enough to drive on the left side of the road on the way to Edinburgh.

The Indian gave her a semi-bow and ~~politely~~ *gallantly waved his hand toward the tiny wheel-house that also served as a sleeping cabin. Along either side, the built-in long cushioned benches could be extended by hinged wings that lay flat to the sides. Pulled out, the wings were supported by 2×4s that Corso had cut to size. Four or five people could sleep here in reasonable comfort. With the food cooler and the extra gasoline in the fifty-gallon drum that was tied down in the stern, and given a gentle sea, this boat, Tiffany realized, could probably reach Cuba. But she wasn't going into the cabin and she shook her head. The other man raised his arms helplessly. The Indian again bent at the waist and motioned her inside. Before they knew it, she whirled about, pushed the dark man in the face, and leaped onto the dock. Years of tennis had made her ankles strong, and she landed in a runner's crouched position, but the Indian had already darted to the side of the boat and vaulted over her head, alighting several feet beyond her, his blunt arms swung wide to shoo her back like a* ~~stray dog~~ *chicken. She saw several people at the ferry berth watching them, and she screamed, "Help me! Somebody help me!" The Indian swept her up in his arms and handed her, kicking and struggling to the other man who dragged her into the cabin, squeezing her breasts and sliding his hand down* ~~between her legs~~ *into her crotch. She bit his hand when he tried to cover her mouth and she was certain that she'd almost severed the last joint of his pinky. He howled and slapped her with unsuppressed glee repeatedly. By now, the watchers at the ferry berth had started running toward them, and the Indian had jumped aboard, started the boat, and brought them swerving out of the bay toward the Caribbean side of the island. Tiffany felt a welt forming on her cheek, her upper lip swollen and bleeding where it had been slammed into her teeth. Her would-be rapist — if that's what he was, if he hadn't merely been trying to get her out of the pubic public eye and was grabbing her wherever he could — was tearfully binding his finger with an unclean handkerchief.*

Trudy had been young and beautiful, adoring her husband's cool wit and the movement of his knowledgeable hands along her body (they should know about this in Oberlin!) and she remembered the frown that pulled her mother's patrician face into a mask of contempt whenever Trudy would say, "You don't understand, there is no age difference between us. In many ways, he's younger than I am. Inside."

"You mean, he's just a boy?" her mother quipped.

"Well, maybe. Like Daddy is. You know how men can be."

"Do I?" her mother offered, drifting away, her back turned, the closed study, where her husband labored at his ineffectual prose, like a ship run aground, with her still on the bridge scanning the night sky.

Trudy remembered the scene between her father and Josh. Her father's tobacco-stained teeth visible as he talked and clenched his pipe between them. He swept his hand aloft in an unexpectedly graceful gesture, then the other one.

"Love is love," he'd said. "Age, I suppose, doesn't matter."

He'd looked at his wife for approval. Tight-lipped but not grim, upright in her chair but not prudish, she had seemed almost jealous at what could have been for her a second chance — had she met her own Josh, had she not grown so comfortable so quickly in the lanky arms of a boyish novelist *manqué*.

It took them half an hour to reach the area of Reef Bay Plantation, where they anchored off-shore for two hours, before a man waved to them from the old settlement that came to land's edge and more than anything else reminded Tiffany of the shore that Conrad's Lord Jim had stood on as Marlow sailed away, leaving Jim behind among his ~~unlettered childish innocents~~ first nation[?] *savages. The Indian started the boat and brought them slowly in. It was Corso on shore, amid signs warning tourists to drink water, not soda, to avoid dehydration. And it was Corso who stepped aboard, shaking his head, disappointed, telling her, "You should not have done that." He produced a knife of the kind used for* ~~reaming~~ cleaning *fish — long, serrated on one side, unspeakably sharp on the other.*

"Now," he said, "we might have to hurt you if you don't behave. You understand?" He pressed the point ~~between her breasts~~ against her throat.

"Take that away," she gasped. "Can't you see I'm already hurt?"

"Ah." He lowered the knife and gently touched her cheek. "We can help that."

He spoke to the Indian, who made his way toward the tourist information hut and broke into it.

"You know," Corso said, "my men would not have done anything to you. They are too afraid of me to ~~flaunt~~ disobey my orders."

But Josh Devereux was cautious about their future and thought of the lake cabin he'd inherited from his father as a fail-safe alternative. "Who knows?" he'd said to her. "At least here we'll always have a place to live." His greatest fear, she now understood, was of being mediocre. Or was it hers? Oddly, it had never bothered her father. She remembered the blood trickling out of Josh's ears and nose. The Morris Minor on its side. Her body pulled by gravity into Josh's, but also by the vacuum his death had instantly created. And now, for some reason, she felt the pain of having lost a sister she'd never seen, whose absence she'd been conceived to remedy, filling the empty space with herself.

With Tiffany Longworth.

The first-aid kit that the Indian returned with had some alcohol, band-aids, peroxide, cotton. She wouldn't allow any of the men to help, touching a wad of cotton to the mouth of the alcohol bottle and patting the welt on her face. My God, she thought, what will happen to me? She couldn't have imagined that she'd spend the next several days in an open-air cottage on the Cinnamon Bay campground, worrying about the falling coconuts as she made her way to the outside toilets, snatching her feet away from the holes of huge spidery land-crabs, sweating at night on her cot as the little electric fan that Corso had brought from Cruz Bay blew the pitilessly dense air toward her, while outside the wild mongooses, brought years ago to the island to deal with rats, fought with and maimed the cats that she would see left half-alive on the floor of the outdoor commissary where she and Corso had breakfast — and where she would finally come to think that it wasn't so bad, any of it, as long as she could be with him, because something in her had given way, that part of her habituated to comfort and the care that ~~health~~ beauty requires. The everyday instinct — which she knew now it wasn't — that urged her well-being as first, foremost, necessary as the sun, had withered away and left behind a thrilling scorn for the safe, the secure, the bourgeois.

She thought back to the years when her income from Josh's estate was being eaten up. At Blessing Lake, her lovers spent their days drinking wine on the dock or driving to a bar on Route 22 in Brewster or waiting for her to finish writing her stories that seemed to them an aberration when she could have the real thing, which they offered frequently. One day she snapped up an armful of Harlequin and Silhouette romances and buried herself in them for two consecutive days, while a lover — Charles, a Nam veteran and at the time a doctoral student in history — busied himself scooping weeds out of the shallows with a newly purchased rake, until he experienced a sudden flashback to the Mekong Delta and the friends he'd lost there. He spent the rest of the afternoon smoking joints, watching a family of Canada geese that paddled from dock to dock and begged stale bread from the summer residents. In the morning, when she awoke, Trudy found no evidence of him. Not even a note.

"All those romances seemed to clear my head," she told Ray years later.

Then her father died. Trudy's mother sold the house in Hartford and moved to Saratoga, to be near some cousins, and to be able to spend part of her summer at Lake George. She became nervous and flighty, renewed old acquaintances, started going to the race track, and though Trudy tried to see her often, her mother seemed to withdraw into a kind of silliness that culminated when she became engaged to a retired art dealer who had specialized in paintings by the pre-Raphaelites. At her father's grave Trudy had felt both sorrow and relief. He'd been found slumped over his typewriter, unshaven, pages strewn across the room.

After the funeral, her mother said, "I burned them. They were terrible. He didn't know what he was doing."

And now her mother was dead. A sudden and swift cancer. Trudy had wept when she returned to the lake cabin from her mother's funeral. She became determined to do well for herself, to write for an audience who would buy books (contrary to her father's notion that the less a book sold, the more likely it was important). She read more romances and then wrote one about a young girl traveling to England, where she met a man like Josh, but with a sinister past, a man whose German wife had mysteriously disappeared on the Continent. And the girl went with him in search of her, ending up in a small village in the south of France, finding the wife besotted with drink and a lover who tried to attack the tall, deft husband, Duncan Heath III. It was no match. Duncan's athleticism was more than appearance. The girl — Hillary — was by then deeply in love with him. When they returned to England, she caressed his brow, smoothed away his cares, and gave her young body into his hands.

Trudy called the book, *A Chest of Jewels*. But the title was changed to *Passion in Velvet* by the third editor she'd sent it to, and she met Ray at a conference, and he wound up winning the modeling contest and posing for the cover after the editor persuaded the publisher of a new series to give Trudy a chance.

"Something different here," he'd said, "even within the usual conventions. Something terribly sad, but romantic."

Ray, who knew all the photographers, and who had a dark room of his own (there seemed nothing he couldn't do with a negative or a document), offered himself in every conceivable way, and Trudy, feeling not so much lonely as simply unattached, at loose ends, indulged herself, taking him with his long hair, smooth voice and habit of smiling while looking off into the distance, never understanding why in the years to follow, after the divorce, they could remain friends, why she didn't move on, why she was content to allow her body the drug, the solace that Ray was, without any connection to the real current of her life. Which was what? But with Ray she'd felt safe, if in some crucial way unnoticed, while her heroines increased their risks book after book, searching for fulfillment.

Corso brought her to a tourist cabin at Cinnamon Bay. It had an electrical outlet and two of its sides were screen walls, allowing air to flow through from the beach, though the cabin was built up against a hill that blocked and repelled any breeze. At night, the hill and surrounding vegetation were alive with small animals and frequent screams. The several cots were soggy and mildewed from humidity. There were two shelves along the cinder-block wall, and below them a worm-eaten red-stained table with two splintery benches. Set in the front screened wall was a heavy door with two locks. Outside, on the cement patio, was an iron barbecue grill bolted to a vertical steel pipe. The roof of the cabin slanted like a lean-to's, allowing the coconuts that fell from the trees to bounce and roll to the ground. Posted on a palm tree that one had to pass on the way to the outside toilets and showers was a sign that invited guests to eat the coconuts but to please dispose of the shells properly. NO LITTERING PLEASE. Tiffany, itchy from no-see-ums and the mental effect of hearing squadrons of drifting, lonely mosquitoes seeking the blood they needed to propagate themselves, stumbled toward the toilets at least twice a day — she held everything in for as long as she could, even though Corso's Indian helper was the soul of politeness and always faced the beach while he waited for her to finish. Corso had warned him to look for writing implements that Tiffany might use to scrawl a message in one of the stalls.

"What?" she said into the phone.

"What do you mean, *what*?" It was Else. "Don't I ever get you in a good mood?"

"I thought it was someone else."

Else snorted. "I wonder who."

"No chance I'll tell you."

"Hah!" Else was not easily put off. In the summers at Blessing Lake, she swam naked every morning to

Trudy's dock and back — sometimes pausing for some of Trudy's coffee while standing shoulder-deep in the water. Later, she would practice her cello, still adjusting to a widowhood that was several years old. Resilient, she had grown close to the other cellist in Frederick's orchestra — Leonard Abernathy, a tall widower from Scarsdale.

Now, Else needed a lift to her cabin, since her car was in the shop. She wanted to rake leaves and clean the property. She lived almost within walking distance, near Columbia University, but Trudy demurred.

"Else, I'm just so involved in this new book."

"Actually," Else replied, "it doesn't matter much. I'm just a little bored. Are you coming to the next rehearsal?"

"I doubt it. You don't think Frederick will care, do you?"

'Darling, anything you do is sacred, even when you ignore him."

They chatted a bit and then hung up, but Trudy was remembering the phone call of the previous night.

"Listen," Ray said, "I hate to ask you, but I'm really short of cash this month."

"What about all that new work you showed me?"

"I wanted you to see what I was doing. My new show won't be until spring. I can't stop working now just to make a few dollars."

"Run out of old girlfriends to mess up the pictures of?"

"Don't be a bitch..."

This morning, after Else's call, her apartment was almost as cool as the kitchen in the cabin at the lake.

A mist rose from the Hudson, and if she leaned over her terrace and peered north, she'd see the George Washington Bridge shrouded in fog, vehicle lights moving like little alien beings. Less than an hour ago, Frederick's cheerful high-pitched voice had come twanging over the phone and she'd suddenly remembered watching him when he was conducting the orchestra at a concert in Maryknoll last spring, dressed in tails, his pants too short, his wrists and white sleeves extruding from his coat. Every time he raised his arms, the coat hiked up and the tails opened, then closed like a long black gill as his arms descended, and dilated again, and closed. His boyish face gleaming, his smile a perfect crescent. But when he conducted, his shoulders seemed broad and powerful, the fingers of his right hand clamped on the baton. And she had been jealous, watching the soprano eye him, nodding, launching Mozart's *Exsultate, juibilate* even as she smiled, the woman's throat pulsing, her dark thick hair swept back from her face and down her back like the sleek fur of an animal freshly into her majority. Trudy had completely surprised herself. Jealous of that singer! Indeed, Frederick was leaning toward the soprano, smiling with more than the acknowledgment of a cue, his eyes lit with sexual energy, his music filling the small church, the relief panels of the Stations of the Cross that lined both walls of the nave depicting in the last scenes a languorous Christ whose waxen androgynous body could have been that of a young male rock star's or a girl's.

"Let's start over," Ray had said soothingly...

She was remembering Frederick withdrawing his cock, sighing, rolling off her as if to turn to his small orchestra and prod them into the next movement. His back damp, his skin soft as a child's. ("Aren't you sweet, Fred." She patted his large rump. Trailed her long-nailed index finger up his groin. Held his exhausted member in her hand. "You are perfectly cute.") He had this time bruised her upper arms with his strong hands and yelped when he discovered what he'd done.

"My God! Why didn't you tell me I was doing that?"

Actually, she hadn't felt his grip. They'd gone to a friend of Frederick's recital at the Juilliard School. And there'd been a reception, where the performers needed praise. "You were great! Wonderful!" (Yes, but in what respect and to what degree? And what were your favorite moments? The cadenza? My phrasing of "*suspire, suspire?*") It was entirely to Frederick's credit that he hadn't sought reviews of his love-making.

Yesterday, Tiffany had been forced out of a cool retreat she'd found for herself. Three wild donkeys had entered the area and come to a halt, perfectly serene in the shade, less than two yards away, ears twitching — watched from a close distance by the Indian in his baseball cap. One of the privileges that Corso allowed her was to sunbathe when the beach was empty and at its hottest, as it was during the middle hours of the day, and now she was hidden among the trees. Late in the evening, he would take her to the edge of a small dune for the breeze and a moon whose glare tumbled through the tropical air. But later, after Corso left, she would have to sleep on the cot flanked by the sleeping forms of the

*two accomplices, their open-mouthed breathing, and
she would long not only for an early sunrise but for the
return of Corso from St. Thomas, where he conducted
business, some of it, she assumed, concerning her.*

"How are you? I should have asked you that first."
Ray's affectation of a concerned, consoling voice jarred
her, as if he'd been eavesdropping... *there was so much
she had to remind herself of, the differences, the cultural
nuances, the...* "so I figured I could ask you..." *...strange
compatibility of their bodies, but the way that money
snaked in and out of his thoughts, she could almost see
it... fanged and... could she ignore...*

"You know," she said, "you still owe me from last
year."

"God," he moaned, "you make me feel like a gigolo."

"You said it, I didn't."

*But there was still no news as to what he was
demanding and she wondered just how much cash she
could raise. She needed clothes. Her current outfits
were sun-bleached and tatty. The frequent and careless
washing of cold-water-only dresses and tops when they
went to town for supplies had created a wardrobe of
baggy, wrinkled fits that made her look like one of the
domestics on the boat to Charlotte Amalie.*

It was good this morning, working almost against
any expectation of a readership. Perhaps it was the full-
page ad in today's *Times* that had featured the life-sized
face of Lila Wentworth Paddington, in which teased-
out blond hair swirled about plumpish features with
the hint of a smirk — globular pearl earrings suspended
like small satellites, her hands folded into each other

in a gesture of victory, a huge sapphire ring reflecting the photographer's flash, and the very expensive watch showing 6:33 P.M. Time for cocktails. It was the eyes, the unintelligent eyes. The woman could have been a checkout girl at the A&P! And the book, described as a treasure to give or keep, was small. Specially priced. Her third. Or was it her fifth? Trudy's own last book had been the victim of a depleted promotions budget, though her agent had hinted at something else, as if they hadn't wanted to throw good money into a book that wouldn't sell anyway. And it hadn't. But it hadn't failed, either. The publisher had made some thousands. But she hadn't earned all of her advance. That was the real failure. In a violent, self-accusatory mood, she'd almost stopped paying her dues to the Romance Writers of America Association. And here was this woman all over the back page of the "A" section, where Trudy never wanted to be in the first place, where publishers put a false and captured face that no real person could ever inhabit.

Now she was remembering her one bad ovary, her twisted fallopian tube, which meant that she and Josh would never have been able to conceive a child, nor would she feel the terror of turning on her own babies without meaning to, an inadvertent Medea, none of that. She remembered how with Frederick, something remote, unknown, had broken loose in her, as he'd hovered over her and she'd bunched the flab of his waist in her hands in a frenzy.

It was the morning after the Indian had slaughtered a chicken behind the tourist cabin that Tiffany begged Corso to explain what he wanted of her.

"He's a Santero," Corso said, pointing to the Indian who was at the moment carrying trash down to the garbage cans at the foot of the hill. "So you mustn't be upset. It's not like Voodoo, you know. He's just worried. He was asking the spirit for help." Tall, deep-voiced, Corso spoke in soothing tones.

"He's worried? Why don't you answer my questions? I still don't know if you intend to hurt me."

She knew even as she said it that she was not in danger, but she hoped that he would volunteer more information if he perceived anxiety in her. She had by now assumed that money was involved. After all, her father was the head of a conglomerate that controlled companies with products as varied as frozen pies, shoes made in Brazil, computer paper, textiles, telephones, and certain unspecified pharmaceuticals. Early on, Corso had verified who her father was, and referred to Thomas Longworth as an American mogul who hadn't the slightest idea of the damage he did. But when Tiffany pressed him for details, Corso always turned moodily away — stared off into the distance at a launch returning to St. John from the island of Tortola or at the incredible stenciling of a setting sun that streaked the sky. She knew instinctively that his painting, his art, and this gloomy turn in his nature were like vines twined around the pole of his life. But it wasn't until this morning that she also understood there was something that personally involved her. Or her father. And she wondered just how long it would take her family to contact the police because they hadn't heard from her or been able to reach her. But she was partly to blame *for that. "I just need to be alone, completely alone," she'd told her mother, that morning in East Hampton, as the sea washed in a gray tide that each year crept ever closer to her parents' deck, her mother's elegant profile lifted in thought, seen against the cloudy day like a cameo ever so slightly yellowed in its jeweled but tarnished setting. "What are you really telling me, dear," her mother asked, "that you have forgotten Jeffery, or that you're trying to? Or that you can't confide in us anymore?"*

Standing outside the Juilliard auditorium at Lincoln Center, Frederick grinned fatuously and kissed Trudy's hand.

"You are so beautiful," he said.

And she was. Finished with writing for the day, she had soaked in the tub, perfuming the water with essential oils that left her skin so smooth she moved through the air without friction or any palpable sense of the elements around her. She hadn't expected to do more work on her book, but now that she had, the freedom it produced in her seemed to fill her spirit, lifting her out of herself. At the same time, her breasts ached and an urgency all through her being startled her as she looked at Frederick. Is it really possible, she thought, to be in love with him?

"I suppose you have a right to know," Corso said. He hunched over the rotted picnic table in the cabin. Just above his tanned forehead was a thin white line created by the border of his yachting cap. He looked vulnerable, like someone in the midst of healing. Or had that not yet begun? Was he in some way still searching for the wound? It seemed too ironic

that she, his captive, should be sympathetic. But she couldn't help it, once he began the story of his sister: the madness that ruined her youth; the Cuban refugee doctor in Miami prescribing an experimental drug produced by a company in the conglomerate overseen by Thomas Longworth; reading about her father who assured the public that there had been a tragic error in the data generated by an outside testing laboratory; that financial damages would be awarded to the patients affected. What, Corso asked Tiffany, could bring his ~~beloved so nearly his twin that it ached to be apart from her when they were children~~ *sister back from the physical grave? Even before her actual death, she had already perished in the grave of her mental illness. Did she, Tiffany, really think that money would console his family for the way his sister had asphyxiated in the middle of the night, gasping through her asthmatically collapsed bronchi?*

With sudden clarity, Trudy felt that Frederick, in spite of his arrant lack of godly physique, had touched her deeply, the sine wave of his touch echoing in a rising and falling, almost tidal but certainly pleasurable sense of herself, beyond the crass approbation of the crowd, *surpassing the cool glitter* of what she'd always seen as the unshakeable edifice of... *now, shining down on her as from...*

"Is this an eye for any eye?" Tiffany asked.

"I thought it should be so," Corso replied. "At first. I was filled with hatred. I could think only of a death, something to crush your father's heart."

"And now?"

He placed his hands together and held them in front of his lips. He stared down at the cracked cement floor of the cabin and sighed heavily.

"Now," he said, "I want to do a portrait of you."

"But why?" She was tired but anxious to talk more, while the Indian was down near the beach, taking his walk.

"I thought I would send it to your father."

"You want money, then."

"No." He clasped his hands behind his back and walked slowly to the screen wall that faced the hill behind the cabin. Out there was a scuffle of small animals, beneath the racket of crickets.

"You want my father to know what you might do to me." She sat on the sagging bed, the unpleasant odor of insect repellent rising from the mattress like chemical sweat.

He turned and faced her. "I did not say that. I would never hurt you." She realized, then, that she had for days now been wanting him to need her.

JANUARY 22 WAS A cold, clear day, the remnants of two previous storms lining the walkway from the parking lot with cindery ice and tamped-down snow, while the pagoda-like tower of the stone Maryknoll seminary building with its roof tiles suggested a warmer climate, one lit by extravagant dawns, bathed in greenish hues. Looking up at the observation area in the tower, one expected a helmeted medieval Chinese soldier to be shading his eyes against the sun as he surveyed the surrounding lowlands for signs of an advancing enemy force.

The Choral Society would be performing four *Magnificat* hymns and a "Hymn for the Dormition of the Mother of God." At rehearsals, Trudy knew there'd been difficulty with the modern piece by Arvo Pärt, some of the violinists sawing away with more hope than expertise, their genial pink countenances so distorted by strain it was almost comical in recollection.

Within the apse of the chapel, wooden folding chairs had been arranged in concentric semi-circles around the orchestra dais that faced the tiers of benches where the singers would file in soon, music in hand, the men in dark suits, the women in black, with white ruff collars. In the eastern end of the chapel, outside the immediate area of the musicians and singers, were the long pews that the Maryknoll fathers filled each morning for services, especially on Sunday, when worshippers from the neighboring communities attended for reasons of faith or curiosity about this building that overlooked the Hudson Valley. One could almost see down to the river, where the correctional facility, Sing-Sing, sadly reduced from its days as the home of the electric chair, seemed to crumble into the water. The high walls of the chapel, the stained glass windows so remote in the clerestory formed by the high nave that the scenes they depicted could not be distinguished, combined with the bas-relief plaques in the aisle depicting Christ's journey to Calvary, to produce in Trudy's mind not so much awe as regret. It was the first thing she'd felt entering the chapel, before looking for her friend Else, who suddenly had been forced to abandon her part in the performance because of severe arthritic pain in her fingers. Looking about the chapel, Trudy was reminded of her mother's failed attempts at piety — humility always crushed by something judgmental, unforgiving. "Your father," she once said, "doesn't believe in God. Not since he came back from the war." Trudy saw in her mother's eyes a dimming sense of disappointment, something more than lost promise or a faded youth.

"Actually," she went on, "I don't think he believes in anything."

"Not even in you?" Trudy had asked.

"Especially me."

Wasn't it wrong to be in his arms, after he'd admitted his hatred of her father? Hadn't he, after all, been the author of all her discomfort this past week, and hadn't he shown cruelty to his men, so that she knew he wasn't just a victim, but someone who could very well begin a new cycle of pain all on his own, creating new injustices by perpetrating them on others? His mouth this moment moving across her nipples was like a circle of flame and her body ached, emerging from its coldness, as from a position she had too long maintained, and she stopped him and explored his chest with her own mouth, his smoothly muscled chest, where she traced the hollow of his sternum with her tongue and felt his hand sliding between her legs, her wetness there like the ~~spilled hope~~ *effluvium of a broken vow. How firm he was, how insistently he pressed against her, how hard the mold of his thigh as he lifted his leg over hers and stroked her hair and held her breasts with the fingers of one hand spread from nipple to nipple, a pianist of love achieving a full octave on the instrument of her ~~bovary~~ body. Perhaps it was only pain that she felt, his suffering invading her like an organism that thrived in the bruised interiors of rejected and forlorn ~~brothers and sisters~~ companions.*

There was Else. With her were two couples, the men former colleagues of her friend Leonard at the Catholic university where he'd taught. One of them — tall, wearing wire-rim glasses, his aspect detached and mournful, his smiling younger wife with hair already gray, belying the age difference between them — said how pleased he was to meet such a famous writer. The other man was frail, his monkish pallor in marked contrast to his wife, who shook hands with Trudy as if she were striking a bargain. Else patted the vacant chair next to her for Trudy to sit down. "Look at him. You'd think he was Leopold Stokowski." She pointed at Frederick who had just positioned himself in front of the conductor's podium, holding both ends of the baton. He stood on tiptoe and scanned the rows of singers, then looked down and took a head count of his orchestra. For a moment, he'd forgotten that a substitution for Else had been made and he did not recognize the young woman with a cello next to the other cellist, Leonard Abernathy, who seemed poised for adventure. Frederick turned to the audience. There, in the last row of chairs, just in front of the baptismal font with its rose marble, was Else and next to her Trudy, bundled in a high-neck ski sweater, wearing tapered leggings, perusing her program. He was pleased when he saw her look up. Aware of his gaze, Trudy blew him a kiss and his entire body prickled with joy, but he nodded sternly and then directed himself to the leader of the choral group, a balding, pink-cheeked former dean of students who, in retirement, was devoting himself to concerts and Rotary luncheons. He smiled and bowed at Frederick, who himself bowed in turn. Both men faced their constituents. Both men lifted their arms, their limp hands all at once straightening into a kind of salute. But it was just practice, since so many of the audience were still arriving. Then Frederick left his little dais and the podium, and retired into the corridor that led into the huge antechamber of the chapel. He slipped behind a heavy maroon drape into a passageway that led to a toilet.

...if she was seeking change, why should it be among so many people alien to her, including the man who... the sun shedding its light in an excess of... permanence... that only now... a heartfelt lack of...

When Frederick returned, he walked briskly to the podium, and the audience, including those in the pews in the eastern end, clapped and whispered, "yes, yes," and several priests beamed, while the faint hum of the heating units seemed a chant already in progress, not as counterpoint but as an irresistible humming behind the lips, dozens of people already spiritually inclining themselves in the afternoon light that passed through the high clerestory windows and transformed itself into a shifting glow of reds and blues.

Their future, if they had any at all, Tiffany thought, might rest on Corso's ability to endure her Americanness, her North Americanness. But then she realized that there would be no family for either one of them, once Corso...but would he?

Amazed by her tender feelings, Trudy watched nearby couples find each other's eyes. Frederick looked superb up there at his podium, his face taut with concentration, his plumpness transformed by the occasion and a new tux into maturity of style, his authority, his genius — however small — in full evidence as he tapped his baton on the music stand and nodded at the choir master who bowed.

Trudy was not very happy that Ray had begged for the $700 he needed for supplies. She'd never expected to get back the other loans, but now she resented all of them. Her weakness. She had needed to remind herself, after she'd finished with Tiffany's adventure, why it was that men in her life took advantage of her. She knew that she encouraged it, and scolded herself, almost hearing her mother's tone of voice, as she asked why, exactly why she had given Ray that money, when any fool could see he would always be a taker, his good looks in decline, the prospects for his art about as sound as the currency of a small republic. But lending the money had made her superior. It had given her a sense of independence.

...she knew her love would always be tethered to the doubtful enterprise of his revenge or his need to control it, but she wouldn't let herself be seen holding up a bank, wearing a beret, an Uzi hung from a strap around her shoulders. Something in her, nevertheless, had fallen away, the life she'd known with such ease, the petty irritations of style and forced congeniality,

the artificial languor induced by a lack of passion, the long, dull catalogue of self-stimulated lovers... If there was a future with Corso, it couldn't be exclusively on his terms. Nor could their love be understood as built on the sacrifice of his sister. And they would live where? How? But that didn't have to matter right away. She knew what she would give up, not for him but for herself. The future would be lived! Not talked about.

Frederick swept his hand aloft. The music began, while the sopranos and altos delivered their text with gusto, the first word, the first *Magnificat* flooding the chapel with the spiritual force of Mary's amazement that she had been selected to incarnate the divinity. Trudy was almost jolted out of her reverie, but as the performance swept along, and the tenors and the basses joined their male resonances to the pious voices of the women, she remembered Ray telling her, "You pretend to rise above it all, but you're just as bourgeois as everyone else!" The chorus was singing the "Hymn for the Dormition of the Mother of God," that appendage to the *Magnificat*, in which Mary sings as she ascends to her son, received into his maternal arms, her dormition, her final sleep now a rounded completion of her spirit's journey on earth. Looking at Frederick's inspired, heated face, his hands that pummeled the air and then swept and swooped like a pair of doves, Trudy thought he had never, never looked so fine.

GET UP

IT BEGAN AS a sensation Greg told himself he had just experienced; so someone must be in the room, and if he opened his eyes, his father would be standing over him, and would prod him again, using the blunt tip of his forefinger to stab him in the temple. "Get up." *One-two-three-four, one-two-three-four.* "Take out the dog." It took him a second or more this morning to think, *Blackie's dead.* And though he was again living home, in Astoria, Queens, in the last decade of the century — in the basement apartment of his parents' attached, one-family house — at least he wasn't sleeping on the sofa-bed in the living room, where his father, Max, used to awaken him each morning, while his grandmother prepared breakfast and his sister Margaret (his *half-*

sister, for the 450th time) was still sleeping and his mother, half-awake, stared at the coffee her own mother had put in front of her.

No, no, that life was that life. Now is the last decade of the twentieth century. Today, Gloriana was arriving with her cello. *Not* to move in. It was as he lay spent on the couch last week that Gloriana had said, "I'm a satirist and satirists can't be serious." She'd smiled (almost his... sister Margaret's smile), (but a cello not a violin, not Margaret's squealing notes). "You look like a little boy there on your back." Gloriana's laughter trailing off in a contemptuous sobbing drone. "Don't match wits with me, Greg."

If he didn't open his eyes. If he remembered his mother Sophie's broad, impassive face in the upstairs window, his father, always wearing his teamster's peaked cap, hair turning white, a growling voice now dry, hoarse. If Greg could just enjoy this Saturday off from his cousin Marty's Insurance agency on Queens Boulevard, where he'd gone after the break-up (*Miriam, "How can you just sit there doing nothing?" His sample case shut up like a stock broker's attaché case, the smell of Scrubbing Bubbles and Windex in their West Side apartment like carbolic acid in that famous story about Venice. And later, when he was moving out, "Why would you go there, Astoria? God!"*). If he took just a few more minutes in bed, before the radio came on, a woman's soft voice enumerating temperatures in Dallas, Denver, Seattle (at least he'd never traveled *that* far. Now anyone could buy over the Internet, where his irrelevance popped up like a menu). If he pulled the blanket up around his legs that had been thrashing all night. If he told himself his return to his parents' home, though he had his own rooms, his own entrance, was something he imposed upon himself, freely, with no implication about Miriam who, after all, had been willing to move out of the apartment they were sharing. If he thought about Gloriana ("We'll talk about love later," her blouse open, her breasts unhoused), whose picture in a pewter frame smiled down on him from the antique end table she'd helped him select (not moving in, no, no), the scent of rosewater drifting across the room from her scarf left on the bureau, so that her presence wafted over him. If his mood were less (Mrs. Weiss, eighth grade, her smile favoring the red-haired brother and sister in the front row, the Kahn twins) *subjunctive*: no video rental overdue at the store on Broadway, around the corner from this house and this basement apartment once lived in by his... sister Margaret, who was now an entomologist, having given up music for bugs. If he didn't ask why he'd let Miriam keep the apartment in Manhattan, why at first he had moved into a furnished room across from Astoria General Hospital in Queens (when he could have slept in the room upstairs that still smelled of his grandmother, or on the living-room pull-out sofa, *stab, stab, stab*), awakened at night by the revolving reds of the ambulance and altercations outside the Emergency Room. If he hadn't seen his girlfriend from his teenage years, Florence Lacella, last week, her arms full, potato chips and pretzels shining forth in their transparent envelopes from the brown paper bags she hugged to herself. If he hadn't been shocked by the immediacy of remembering the two of them in her parents' living room, soul-kissing on the couch, the winter Olympics and hissing skis on TV, the ski lodges, the steam knocking in her mother's radiator like the puttering out of snowmobiles pulled up to the log building, her skin smelling of saffron.

He was sure it was saffron.

Within seconds he was on his feet, doing fifty runs, touching his toes. In the bathroom, he washed his face vigorously, brushed his teeth, pulled down the skin beneath his left eye. Pink aliveness. It was like the membrane around his heart. He pulled back the foreskin of his penis. Everything clean. Clean. On their first date, Gloriana had said, "Teach me how." In the flickering glare, the sound turned low, squeals and grunts of the video lovers audible, they lay naked on the bed. She asked if he thought those people were aware of the camera on them. If they were sincere. Now she wanted to leave her cello at his apartment, to practice there on Saturday afternoons. There was no room in her parents' home, since she'd moved back in with them.

Sitting at his little kitchen table, Greg severed the fibers of a pink grapefruit with the serrated knife. He allowed the tart meat of the grapefruit to cool his tongue that lately he had been pressing into the roof of his mouth. If he allowed his tongue to go limp, it lifted itself, trembling. This morning's fried egg (the slick, membrane-covered yolk, the soft round body of the unborn) that he now penetrated with a corner of whole wheat toast was an attempt to reinstate the old Greg, whose mouth did not fill with saliva when he held his tongue motionless. The Greg who used to open a sample case and dissertate on his products.

He brushed his teeth again, washed the dishes, picked up the brown video case containing the tape that had scenes of men entering women from behind, slapping the women's buttocks so that a redness like chapped skin appeared. When Gloriana asked if she could slap him there, he'd said, "Certainly not." When she said, "Then do me," he refused. He'd kept the tape an extra day, intending to watch it alone. But now he was glad to return it, wondering what the woman behind the counter thought, while her teenaged daughter, a blond girl working part-time, ripe in her T-shirt (flutter, smile), thanked him.

The BMT elevated train clattered into its Broadway stop. He again saw Florence Lacella. She'd remained thin and still walked with her feet pointing outward. Opposite the stationery store, she stared, then cupped her hand over her mouth, then smiled (dimples, the dimples). "Imagine that," she said. Her blue eyes, as in the past, still strayed from the face of the person she spoke to, looking over the person's shoulder, then into his eyes, then away. Greg rolled his eyes (an old tic, a saccade in search of a text), jerked his head to one side, and tried to laugh. He remembered that it was she who had pursued him when they were fifteen. He'd sit on the curb, looking away, while she tousled his hair. She liked to talk about her day at school. When her father died, she wept quietly against Greg, and he feigned sympathy when all he felt was repugnance. He didn't care how she felt. His own mother had just told him that Max was her second husband. Her first husband, Greg's real father, had died young. He didn't want Florence on him. "Imagine that." Donald, once his best friend, now her husband, worked for the phone company. Two children, boys. Yes. Well. "Imagine that."

GLORIANA SAID, "IT'S unfair." She sat on one of Greg's three kitchen chairs, the cello upright between her legs, the bow dangling from her left hand. She plucked a bass note, and frowned. "Mother wanted a girl and got me — uh! — because father didn't care. He just had no force." Her eyes wavered and she pushed her glasses further up her nose. "And don't tell me about babies." Her lids fluttered and her indulgent smile reappeared. "Aren't you afraid of babies?" She executed several thrums on the cello, imitating the sound track of a silent film. She grinned, her lips pressed flat, her eyes shut. She and Greg had met at a Wednesday evening Adult Education business course at William Cullen Bryant High School, the final exam for which they both ignored, after their first date on New Year's Eve (her low-cut dress, a yellowish warmth extending to her throat, her mother and father nodding shyly. He shook their hands, taking in the mother's shoulder-length white hair, the red-brown Indian face. The father tall, light-skinned, with a postage-stamp black mustache. Employed as a shipping clerk. Disappointed by Gloriana's withdrawal from college. He was always shaking his finger at her. "Education. Education." Her mother asking, "Are you happy, Ginger?" using her nickname).

It was the second week she'd been coming to the apartment, leaving the cello with him. (Greg was relieved to be away from Miriam's vegetarianism, her soft tones that had seemed so sympathetic, her lank hair and complacent artiness in their apartment on West 83rd Street, her poetry readings. She'd been drawn to his dark good looks, but discovered that his narrow face and prominent eyes, at first so poetic, were just the paper-thin covering of an ordinary soul. Then his company folded.) Now he wondered how Gloriana could ever be self-supporting, losing jobs at the rate she did. She had worked in McDonald's. She'd lasted two months as an office temp, a job that concluded when she was caught writing sly notes to accompany correspondence. She'd clerked at Barnes & Noble. (Miriam worked at Shakespeare & Co., on Broadway, the store extending down 81st Street, its literary criticism section the noisy floor above a tiny repertory theater in a basement below — the theater where Miriam had taken him to see pieces by Beckett: a large room draped in black, the seats black, the production of *Footfalls* allowing only a crack of light as a robed woman paced back and forth, a voice asking, "Will you never be done revolving it all?" And Miriam in black, invisible in that airless place.)

Gloriana had just taken a part-time job with a photocopy store. Though Greg was sure his mother looked down from her window every time Gloriana walked up the driveway and knocked on the door and later used the key he gave her (*not* moving in, not), his parents had said nothing about his guest. And again, last Saturday night, he'd not been able to penetrate her. Gloriana's hymen, intact, could not be broken. In a desperate moment, and with her consent, he had tried to penetrate her with the eraser end of a new #2 pencil, with no result. A muscular wall resisted him. She protested that his efforts did not hurt and that he should continue. He found himself sitting on the floor, dazed, his erection wavering, his face flushed. She said, "Oh, silly, come here, right here, by me." She patted the mattress. And pulling the blanket over them, she took him in her mouth. Later, in the dark, as he sat on a kitchen chair, opposite where she lay supine on the bed, she chatted while she masturbated. Though she had already brought him to climax, he was annoyed that she was accomplishing the same thing for herself. He seemed to have no part in it.

THE SNOWFALL IN the first week of February was deep and Greg was feeling poorly — a lingering, low-grade fever, his throat scratchy. Last week, when he'd come home to find the canisters disturbed on his kitchen counter, he deduced his mother had been in to clean. Or snoop. (In childhood, his... sister Margaret kept insects in jars and fed them moldy table scraps. Their mother washed floors every other day, making them gargle Listerine, always spreading the smell of bleach and pine oil.) When he'd gone upstairs to pay the rent, he asked his mother politely if she'd been in the apartment. She threw up her arms, sat down, aggrieved by his accusation, and wept. His... father Max said, "How could you?" Then Max coughed unpleasantly, phlegm rushing to the surface, but Greg didn't know if his... father was talking to him or to his mother.

And there was the scene with Gloriana. She told him why she'd been almost expelled from college before she dropped out. A woman instructor, an overbearing, flat-faced blond, had complained about her behavior, the way Gloriana would stand up in class or leave without permission and then come back in. "Life in this culture will be very difficult for you," the woman had said. Then Gloriana slapped the woman's face. "We argued about truth," she told Greg. "That fat old blond doesn't know any of my truth." She laughed. "I hope you don't tell *him* everything I tell *you*," she said. Greg thought she meant his penis. So he snickered. But Gloriana sat with the cello between her knees, gloomily tuning it, ignoring him.

Greg had been feeling low since then, and now with the snow, his fever began to bloom into something flu-like and delusional. He'd confessed as much to Gloriana on the phone. When she arrived with a paper bag filled with things, he felt relief (but for some reason was remembering Miriam asking him, "Do you think ghosts have genitals?" It was the first time he'd observed something unreasoned in her. Something weird. "God, you have no sense of humor!"). But it was no funnier than his mother telling him as he graduated high school that Max wasn't his real father.

Gloriana made him lie down, saying, "Baby's sick." She made a long crooning sound (*Miriam humming to Schumann's Lieder. Her black stockings. Her Kahlo T-shirt. Her lips against his ear, as if for endearment.*

"I'm leaving you, Schatzie.*"*) He heard familiar sounds, Gloriana pouring something into a saucepan, heating it. Then he heard a pop as of rubber tubing turning inside out, a cap squeaking and being screwed tightly into place. She kept her back to him, turned, extinguished the light, and approached his bed. He heard the loosening of her clothes, their soft collapse to the floor, and as she approached, and leaned over him, he inhaled the sweet odor of her body, giving off its heat as companion to his fever. She offered her breasts that in the dark, by instinct, he found, burying his face in them, kissing, muttering, while she soothed and stroked his febrile chest. Then Greg heard the pop of rubber again, and she was saying, "Poor baby." She closed his hands over the warmed baby-bottle and pushed it toward his mouth. "Take it," she whispered. "Take it. You'll feel better." For an instant he held the nipple to his mouth. Then he pushed her from him. "Go away! Are you crazy?" He leaped out of bed, dragging the blanket, standing now by the front door, staring through the small diamond pane of glass at the snow gathering in the driveway. He pulled the blanket around him, his face hot with shame, fever, his feet emerging cold between the tip of the blanket and the floor. He said, "I can't do this." "Are you angry?" she whispered. That she was hurt, or could be hurt, had not occurred to him. He was dizzy. And disgusted. She left, late as it was, and in the snow.

IN THE FIRST week of March, Greg's... father had his larynx removed. Max's sore throat and hoarseness had been diagnosed as cancer. Greg's mother merely shook her head whenever Greg and Margaret (by telephone) (blond hair, something of their mother's impassive face, their... father's blue eyes) tried to convince her that Max had plenty of future. Early diagnosis. A lightning surgery strike. And the little white flap Max would wear over the hole in his throat, from which his esophageal speech would issue, that croaking, dry parody of Max's former growl — it would be like an eye patch. But all their mother could imagine was changing the wet gauze. She shuddered. She'd heard about men who smoked cigarettes through a button-sized aperture in their throats. When she wasn't crying, she stared into corners, or scrubbed her kitchen counter until her arms gave out. The possibility of using an electronic device that looked like a remote control box for the TV, something Max could press against his throat that would produce a robotic voice not unlike the voice in the automated subway at the Atlanta airport ("The train is leaving the station. Please hold on") that Greg had once traveled on, Max would not consider. He wrote on the white pad kept near the bed, "I don't want to sound like a machine." Once outside the room, Max's wife collapsed into her (*yes!*) son's arms. The attention his parents required would come mainly from him, since he lived below, and since Margaret's work mandated travel to places like Costa Rica and she was busy with the children of her friend Klaus (there was talk of Eastern Europe, Prague). Greg found himself dreaming of Margaret. He'd awake remembering her long legs, his... sister in her underwear, Max scolding that she was too old to run around like that. Greg remembered how he'd think about her as he slept on the couch, waking with an erection that wilted when Max began prodding him, *one-two-three-four, one-two-three-four*, "take out the dog."

Gloriana had begun to suggest that Greg was involved with someone else. She intimated that Greg reported on her activities. That he was in league with a former teacher of hers. When Greg confided to Marty in the insurance office — careful to keep his voice low, so the secretary Mrs. MacMillan couldn't hear him — that his sex with Gloriana was mostly oral — with some digressions toward the anus — Marty, a little embarrassed, said, "That's great." Then he said that business was very slow. They'd have to pick things up somehow, get more clients. Leaning over his desk toward Greg, built like all the men in Max's family, Marty showed muscular arms even through his shirt sleeves, the definition that comes from four days a week at the gym. He seemed menacing. Greg nodded and tried to puff up his old enthusiasm, the kind he had on his old job when he'd boasted he could sell solar roofing to the homeless in cardboard shelters.

But Greg watched more videos than ever. He discovered other rental stores. Everything he did, after all, was legal. And people made a living from it. This woman, who fetched videos from their shelves behind the counter, went home to cook dinner. Watched inane family programs in the evening. And in some quiet moment, when the children were asleep, she took her man in her mouth. Thinking about these things, he was prone to small accidents, like dropping his coffee cup at the office. No matter what he attempted in their love making — anal intercourse, his cunnilingus — Gloriana merely giggled, though she would occasionally lean back and say, "Make love to me, Greg, show me how." It was always Gloriana who brought herself to climax. He seemed to be an instrument of her fantasy and he was beginning to feel wrong. Something was wrong everywhere. Sales were declining. People were cutting back on their policies. Stocks were sluggish. There were rumors of federal and state cutbacks.

Twice a week, Greg visited his mother and Max, offering to bring take-out food that his mother always forbade. "You never know what they put in things." In the beginning, Max would nod, point to the white pad hung from a string around his throat, and lift his hands as if to say, "What can I do?" In spite of Greg's protests, his mother made dinner, something mild and easily digestible, and they all watched TV for a couple of hours. Greg detested the news programs and documentaries they were addicted to, and once Max became adept at esophageal speech and less shy about how it sounded, his words articulated from the hole behind the gauze sounding belched and alien, Greg found himself once again chewing his tongue. He began to dread the consequences of constantly chafing himself in this way. Cancer. When he went down to his apartment, he switched on one of his videos and fell asleep amid the muffled gasps, convinced that everything was feigned. One morning, his back stiff, the tip of his tongue sore from a night of catching it between his front teeth, he looked at himself in the mirror. He seemed so haggard. A darkness beneath his eyes. A kind of V where his eyebrows habitually contracted in a frown. He realized he'd sunken into a routine that had not improved.

GLORIANA HELD HIM to the Tuesdays and Thursdays she came to practice cello, something his mother began to comment on. And he'd seen Florence Lacella twice more, once on the corner of Broadway, and once, incredibly, in her copy service job on Queen's Boulevard where he'd quite at random stopped to make a photocopy of someone's term policy. When she smiled at him across the counter, his heart fluttered. He flushed. He was so stricken he had difficulty speaking. All he could manage was, "Well, well." Something in the intelligent movement of her hands, the friendly light in her eyes, her competence as she instructed a girl how to produce two-sided copies, created in him a longing. He remembered how she had pursued him. He wanted her back. But he recalled how Donald had slapped him in the face when they'd argued over a safe call at third base. His best friend. "Listen," he said, "why don't you and Donald join me for dinner some night?" Florence smiled her usual smile and said she'd ask Donald. She exchanged telephone numbers with him. He left almost happy for the first time in weeks. But there had been no call and he looked worn out.

"LET'S JUST CALL him Professor Y," Gloriana said. She had finished playing something resonant by Saint-Saëns and decided to confront Greg. "You know who

I mean. Of course." She tilted her head back, lifting her face to the light, her eyes closed. Something flat in her features, something too serene, the drone of her voice oddly matched to the tone of her instrument. She looked bedraggled. "Oh, Greg, you know. How often do you write him? Just tell me that." He wondered how much of all this was a joke, like the baby bottle. But she told him about Professor Y teaching journalism in an evening course she'd been taking at LaGuardia Community College. "You'd think he was in some kind of *Castle*!" After praising her writing, Professor Y had suggested a liaison that she rejected. He began to fail her work. She accused him. There was a scene. She left the course. But Professor Y left little messages for her everywhere, confessing his love for her, sometimes in the editorials of the *Times* or on subway posters. Her mail, at her parents' apartment, had been steamed open, read and resealed.

One night, tired of being pursued, she met Professor Y at the college after his class, told him to leave her alone. He pretended not to know. Using a ruse, she obtained his telephone number from the department secretary and called him. She found out his home address and stood outside his apartment building in the east Sixties in Manhattan and accosted him, when his arms were full of groceries (he loved potato chips. Greg thought of Florence, her grocery bag full, his heart empty). Finally, there was an episode with the police. "How he *acted*," she said. "As if I couldn't see through him. The way I see through you." Greg felt a great heaviness. She smiled at him, seeming relieved, pleased with herself, and came to where he sat, pressed his head against her womb. "Poor baby," she said. "I'm not angry with you." (All he could think of was his mother saying, "You know, Max loves you like his own son." And the evening he told his... sister he'd been adopted by Max, and she'd said — blond hair falling over one side of her face, thighs gleaming from a day at the beach — "But *I* love you. You're my *brother*.")

THE NEXT MORNING, Greg's mother was at his door. Max was spitting blood. She kept making fists and hammering at the air, at an invisible barrier, biting her lower lip, and stamping her foot as if crushing an insect, though she continued to stare at something behind him, as if the problem were there, in the framed photo of Gloriana. When he got upstairs, he saw the cherry moistness of his father's lips, like those of a boy who'd been kissing too long, but the pallid cheeks, the trembling hand, the near gargle of Max's attempt at speech threw Greg into a dead calm, a nerveless efficiency, as he told his mother to call the doctor. If no one answered, they'd go to the Emergency Room at Astoria General. For the first time in weeks, his head was clear. His father was hemorrhaging. There were things to do. He looked up at the hung photo of Max standing in front of the company's tractor-trailer, eyes squinting in the sun like a sniper's. He stopped his mother from giving Max water. "Maybe we shouldn't do that." "But what else can I do?" Max waved her off. Greg said, "See? We don't know." The doctor told them to meet him at the hospital.

Once there, they walked down a long corridor where several people were stalled on gurneys, an old man with his knees bent, wrinkled shanks exposed, his backless gown hiked up, a woman lying on her back, moist hair in disarray, wisps of it stuck to her forehead, one hand behind her pillow as she stared at the ceiling, her pose nearly erotic. They passed by the small admitting office, Max pressing the pad against his throat, Sophie saying, "Don't talk. Don't try to talk." On a long bench were two policemen, and between them a thin, wild-looking man in his thirties who looked at Max, muttered something, and began to laugh. He bent over and continued to laugh softly. Greg said, "Hey, fuck you! Shut your mouth." The policeman with the blotchy face told him not to pay any attention. The man was here for psychiatric observation. He had just dropped his pants in a grocery store and had walked out onto Broadway to wait for a bus. And now he was singing something Greg recognized from Janis Joplin. Or was it the Stones? Gloriana was right. He didn't know anything about music. All he wanted now was to smash this pitiful fool in the face. "Just watch your mouth," he said, wagging his finger.

Dr. Biondi arrived and examined Max and told them it was to be expected. The throat, reacting to radiation therapy, would bleed from time to time. But they'd been right to call. Greg realized he was two hours late for work. He thought with relief of his job, his neat little desk, the harsh, dependable Mrs. MacMillan, who threatened to throw out anything not in its proper place, while she tended the coffee maker and showed Greg how many errors he'd committed today in spelling or usage. ("Their going to see." "Wo'nt." "A person misses their place." Missus MacMillan.)

The following Saturday, Gloriana was waiting for Greg in the apartment, having used the key he'd given her soon after their first date. He had just come back with a new video, but finding her there, he felt dispirited. "I think I'm pregnant," she said. Sitting down, he began to laugh, lowering his head to his knees. Irritated, she said, "You think this is a joke? You and *him*?" Greg sat back in his chair. They were back to Professor Y. "It's just not physically possible for you to be pregnant, Gloriana! Are you nuts?"

"How do you know so much?" she said, roused to a kind of anger he'd not seen before, though she didn't look at him in any direct way. Her face flat, golden-toned, Asiatic, raised to the light, her eyes closed. "Afraid of little nigger babies?"

"Hey, fuck you!" He was yelling.

"I'm going to kill myself, Greg. I really am. Are you going to help or not?" She opened her eyes and smiled at him demurely.

"What about your cello?"

"Oh, you can have that. You can have everything. You and *him*. You always had all of it, anyway. What chance did *I* ever have?"

"How can you be pregnant?"

"You know, Greg, you just don't believe enough in me. I mean my power. Uh!" She became annoyed, turned away from him, raised her face again to the light. "You think everything is the body. You're just so... dumb. How do you know I'm not inside you the way you are inside me, after I do you?" She laughed.

He yelled, "Okay. Do it, just do it! Kill yourself!" He demanded she get out, wanted her to take the cello, but allowed her to leave it until next week, feeling stricken himself as he watched her meander dejectedly down 32nd Street toward the bus stop. He had suddenly broken up with her. At least it wasn't like wondering with Miriam how he had failed. She had only herself to blame.

HE TOOK A hot bath. His body flushed and tingling beneath his terrycloth robe, he inserted a video and laid back to think how many were the women he'd known. He used present tense and changed *were* to *are*. "Are." A vague memory of something he'd read on *is* — man in white lab coat offering cardboard roses, allergic people sneezing at them — stirred, turned, flickered. A small star in his mind receded. Memory. *Is*. He salivated from a gland, but who would know? Who would know it was him this minute shifting the forces of nature? Letting the saliva gather in his mouth, swishing it through his teeth, imagining the froth of it turning upon itself, while Florence Lacella, his almost wife, was (under pink blankets) turning in bed at this moment, and now his saliva reflected (stop. change.) (corresponded to) the disturbance of air caused by her shifting body: because whether she knew it or not, Florence was connected to him across all of Queens. And the plump woman in the video, on all fours, looking at him over her shoulder, could be Gloriana. Or Florence ready at last to receive him ("Do!"). Or to take Donald in her mouth

He needed something. (*his... sister Margaret, a bug in her mouth, "See how it can live in there?"*)

Getting up, he rummaged through the small drawer he'd given to Gloriana for her odds and ends, and found a pair of panties. He put them on, stroked his silken buttocks, moved his hand down into his crotch, then up over his stomach and chest. He didn't know if what he felt was an autistic (something); a ripple from the air around her bed (*"it's me, Florence," he said. "It's Greg"*); a slow vibration of disappointment, where, in the apartment on Ditmars Boulevard she shared with her husband and two children, Florence (formerly Lacella) Murphy leaned against that husband, Donald, formerly Greg's best friend. And Donald was odorous and sour, half-asleep, breathing noisily after a night of drinking. Florence's stream of desire was now aimed at him, Greg, this very minute where he lay on his back, bulging in his panties. Or was he, this minute, causing her to remember his tongue exploring the cavity of her mouth years ago in her mother's apartment, just as Donald was waking up and inserting his own? But what could occur without Greg's presence somewhere? How could Florence have ever forgotten him? How could she not be thinking of what they'd had, and what they'd missed having?

He rolled out of bed again. In the video, a thin brunette woman was on her back, a dark-haired lover licking into her cavity, the music rising to a tinny crescendo. The image of his father, gauze on throat, was so vivid, he turned, expecting Max to be there, as if he were in his father's video. Everyone watching everyone else. He felt his excitement wane. He stroked his buttocks. Then found himself at Gloriana's drawer again, withdrew the tube of lipstick, and smeared his lips with the purplish tint she said was almost right for her. And for Florence?

He lay back on the bed. Slid off his panties. Donald's hand, on its way to Florence's V, the hand suspended in the air, and Florence's intake of breath keeping her lungs full and frozen, because he, Greg, would not allow the next movement to occur (*Miriam, "You don't have to leave, I will." Someone else's semen trickling down her thigh.*) He held them all fixed in time, his mother weeping. Just now he was causing Donald to ask Florence how often she thought of Greg. A trick, after (do) all. What *is*? Even when he made love to Gloriana, such as it was, his hands sliding over her hips, what proof had he at that moment either of them were real? His erection inattentively languishing while Gloriana reminisced about mother washing her *there* in the bathtub, age four, little Ginger (hot, slippery).

(Respond.) If Florence were not thinking of him, but causing Donald to caress her; if he telephoned her now and she lifted the yellow Princess receiver to her lips and he asked her what Donald was doing. If he said *shhh shhh* when he heard her groan. To hold her... (reorder. conjugate.) *Was*. What might not enter with his semen? (He'd call in sick tomorrow.) Oh, now he'd lost his place. And it was dark. He could not argue away time, the blue fog of it, the cars rustling past on 32nd Street, sound of silk brushed over the back of a chair (cool). His turning down the sound of the TV had no effect on the glow of objects in his room, nor on the traffic lights of Broadway, where Gloriana must be waiting for the bus.

Fixed. The pausing of Donald's hand above. (pubic bristles) (showing through Miriam's leotards) Failure. Or will. *Someone's* power. He'd challenge this dimming, this falling off, this drift of nerves (hands floating away from his wrists, his penis detached, revolving free of gravity, suspended like an astronaut's ballpoint pen). No longer his. He groaned. Somewhere he was in error. ON hER PARenTS' CoUCH, iN bRA AND panTIEs. It floated back into place. Do. Gloriana there in the video he and Florence watch together (*Margaret rolling that wet bug around in her mouth, letting it slip between her lips into her hand*), a strange man entering Miriam, mother still weeping. And the dry, croaking sound from behind the flap on Max's throat. Ah, slippery the world. Lubed. Finally. He would. He would.

GODARDESQUE

For Michael Bolner

A PIECE OF LINT

They are sitting in the diner on stools, facing the mirror in which her face is blurred by steam. His face is never seen. There is a piece of white lint — or is it a crumb? — on his coat, between his shoulder blades. It is always in view, even as she turns to him and says she must leave him. Sometimes he is her husband and they have a child at home being watched by her mother. Sometimes he is just her lover, Paul or Roger. Her face is taut with youth and need, though her abbreviated black Cleopatra wig fits her head badly, not ruining her beauty entirely but giving it a desperate quality that will be more pronounced in hotel rooms with clients. It is not clear yet that she will be doing that, since all she wants is to be on her own, which is why she takes the job in a Sam Goody's music and movie store, where she works part time and is already $200 in debt, the sound track constant and sad. No one knows to whom she owes this money. No one knows who owes her money but is not paying, so that finally she leaves this job for something that pays better. Whatever happened to her husband or lover is not as important as the grooming of her wig and the run-down condition of her little apartment with its river view. She meets a friend her age, just as pretty, nicely dressed, though her make-up is a trifle exaggerated, but she's tidy and clean, not an ordinary streetwalker. The friend tells her how easy it is, renting her body to a client. Not *herself.* The music picks up its beat. A man's falsetto brings with it a lyrical longing and images of flowers on the embankment. The friend leaves her in some neighborhood, but it's not clear where that is, where she is now soliciting — somewhere along Eleventh Avenue, talking to the drivers in cars waiting for the traffic light to change, perhaps Chelsea, on a corner of Eighth Avenue, maybe in the theater district, on 46th Street, off Broadway, or further uptown, where her whiteness is less and less common. She's now with her first client, a middle-aged man indifferently undressing as she stands there smiling in a less painful way than one would expect. He tries to kiss her on the mouth, but she averts her face again and again, so that all he kisses is her hair or the back of her neck. Never her lips. His tongue never able to bring its urgent speech into her mouth. One assumes she doesn't do blow jobs. Unless that is seen as so impersonal that she does it without any sense of invasion or compulsion. But to have a man's mouth on hers, to allow his tongue to contaminate her own, to infuse however strangely his nascent speech into her being — because the mouth, the throat lead to what is innermost — that is the beginning of ideas. That is how his ideas smother her own. That is how damnation or death enter the soul. That is how even angels corrupt. Mouth to mouth. One portal of the pneuma to the other. A cock in the mouth is nothing compared to that. But this is too vulgar to contemplate and probably all she worries about is the sturdiness of the condom and the cold sore on her upper lip. Because she can do a blow job with a condom in place. Or let the man enter her anus as long as she is lubricated and he wears a condom. It's all about the quality of latex and how lucky it is that she is not allergic to it. Still, none of these issues are as conspicuous as her need to be an actress or to send money home if she has a child and is not leading an altogether solo life. Nothing touches her innocence and her wide-eyed smile and coy inclination of the head. What is there to fear? Men adore her. Especially the man filming all this, whose child she has already lost in a miscarriage, which is one reason why she might have had a child at the beginning whom she is leaving behind. There are so many causes for events that truth is less important than what one desires to be the case. And making it so. Which is all she is doing, after all, making her case for pleasure and income and clean sinks and how one emerges basically unadulterated. Unpenetrated by an alien tongue. Which is why that piece of lint, always in the center, always clinging, even now, so many tableaux later, somehow transferred to her and aligning itself with the threads of her black sweater and surviving the random caress of strangers, that lint is now the seed of regret that will bring a bleakness to her love-making in hotel rooms (though nothing could be as dismal as the men removing shirt and trousers and folding them neatly as if getting ready for a physical), that lint the indissoluble crux of how the laws of physics surround the emotional with entropy even in its smallness and indifference, the very thing she dare not brush off as if it were the past. But if the lint is just a crumb from breakfast, a crumble of baguette that dropped from a plate as she passed by her husband or lover and clung to the back of his coat and then transferred to her sweater when she leaned against him in the street, facing away, back to back, looking in the direction opposite to the one he was going while waiting for a traffic light (at a place where she will later be streetwalking), this food particle, the image of sustenance still available in the hunger she is only just beginning to feel, the emptiness, the aloneness of the body, her beauty a kind of vapor that condenses on mirrors from time to time, as in the very first scene — then the narrative moves from clothing (though the lint might have been from a chenille bedspread or a bath towel) to food, from the external to the internal, from beauty to visceral dreaming, and it's time to enter the café where her friend's pimp Raoul or Ralphie or

Milo is playing pinball, watching how the ball is propelled by the spring he lets loose, and who wouldn't believe this is just her, bouncing from one neon bumper to another, only now there's a list and a price, as her fate wobbles and careens through one *ding-ding* after another, her freedom existing in the moments between, when there is neither sound nor flash, and the pimp's hand hesitates as he leans toward her for a kiss, which she allows, unafraid but keeping her lips closed. Alas, he is handsome, protective, though when she asks if he is happy, he shrugs, goes through the client list, checks off her name, sends her to the hotel, and as she waits there is no evidence of needle tracks on her slender arms, no marks of ruin on her still perfect face, no sign of angel dust, smack, meth, crack, no demon in the small closet, no policeman producing his badge as she begins to disrobe, though she never reveals more than her bare shoulder and no one sees any sign of a vaginal discharge or herpes or syphilis, it being the time before AIDS and therefore manageable, so there is no reason to believe her clients are run down or diseased or tortured by obscene compulsions, unless one includes the episode when she goes from room to room down the hall to find another girl willing to help out, and whatever the girl does when she comes back it is off camera — evidence that the client is willing to siphon off his more objectionable needs, leaving everyone-knows-who still intact in her untongued virtue. But why should clients not have their own perversions that fill the statistical blanks in a reality ever shifting and propelled by the pimp's sprung handle, if it wouldn't be heretical to think of God that way (promoting vice and pleasure in the same motion of His hand), and get someone burned at the stake, believing in the first wave of heat, the first blisters on the arms and face, that divinity combusts when love reaches a certain temperature? This brings the issue back to innocence in the midst of necessity (her unnamed childhood, her not-illustrated years at school), the bruises on her arms a kind of determinism, though they resemble the shape of the pimp's finger tips and who wouldn't believe that he could have been dissuaded from such a *physical* course, until she turns her face to the camera and exhibits boredom, a bland intelligence, a childish pout, her full lips that would be unimaginable in the kissing and perusing of a client's body, not to mention his lips, not to credit the entering in his mouth of her own tongue to explore the philosophy of aspiring lust. Still, someone follows her with his camera, and whether the pimp writing his income down in a spiral notebook is a divinity or God is the big-eared stranger in another café who promulgates the equivalence of words and thought so that all she lacks really is the correct vocabulary, one can only speculate that the ending in which she is shot by other pimps trying to buy her from Raoul or Ralphie or Milo (though this appears to be unintentional, the real target being Raoul or Ralphie or Milo, and when the first bad pimp finds his revolver empty and assigns the shooting to his companion there seems an element of accidental mercy) points to the essential lack of survivability in a woman who refuses to be changed or controlled by experience, when all that is is what she's being told it is. She must be destroyed. The piece of lint removed. The crumb eaten.

TENDERNESS
Not that a girl of eighteen with a modified page-boy black wig would know it as more than a shy grin and his hand reaching for hers, unless one counts the three of them in bed — the girl, Paul, the girl's friend Catherine with the freckled face — and Paul asking if he can put his hand there, down there between the girl's legs, while Catherine is asking for a little quiet and no movement on the mattress, as Paul is rubbing the girl's clit, and Catherine knows this and is getting excited because she's been seen stroking the girl affectionately in the movies with Paul on the other side of the girl, that time he leapt up to complain about the speed the film was being run at, as if anyone watching would or could know the difference, looking at this Swedish porn that never showed anything except a girl with her head going down over a man's crotch but out of view and then coming up, though it might as well have been a doctor's office and she was just picking up an earring that had fallen off her left ear, that post still not soldered right. But later, Paul — his name must always be Paul for reasons or origins never explained — recently back from a tour in Iraq, wants to know about birth control, what women are using, as the girl goes demure and turns away, though her friend Elisabeth says (Paul is interviewing her in his new job as a pollster) the girl takes her temperature

every night for signs of ovulation, implying perhaps the girl is using nothing, though Elisabeth herself refers to the *things* a woman can put inside herself like a diaphragm or an IUD that in some women can be grown over and become part of the womb and impossible to extract. No one mentions condoms, they are so obvious. There are the hormone pills. The subcutaneous injections. The morning-after pills. Or, she says, smiling, a curtain rod. Then we see Paul with his friend Charles, also back from Iraq, though part of his right foot was blown off by an IED and in spite of a prosthetic extension on the foot walks with a slight limp. Charles adores the freckles on the girl's friend Catherine's face and wants to know what she's like in bed, on the other side of the girl, while Paul and the girl are having at each other. Paul says stop playing with yourself, will you? Just ask her what you want to know. If she likes you, though why, I couldn't guess, you're so sloppy all the time, you need a shave, you smell. And he laughs. And Charles laughs. They light a joint. In comes the girl fresh from her recording studio, where she's been doing a single as the reborn *yé-yé* girl, a kind of French Brittney Spears, only more innocent these days what with Brittney's bloated body and sons puking in the back of her SUV. But that seems libelous, so let's say the girl is just younger than Brittney and though technically not a virgin still innocent. Just look at that smile. The dimples. The guileless eyes. The always sympathetic regard. The anti-war sticker (*THIS ENDLESS WAR*) on the bumper of her Honda Civic, and how she holds the cap of the aerosol paint spray container as Paul sprays his anti-Bush slogans on the wall of the local church. But no one years from now will understand why these young people can't just get a nice job and get married and get an apartment and pretend it's 1955, the leap forward to 2005 just a different syntax, a dream of women in kerchiefs and burkas a cultural error as the wrong needs get into the wrong heads. Whereas men and women are the same as always. Which is what Paul is trying to figure out, in his interviews, the teenagers around him jittery from Red Bull caffeine drinks, not PCP, because decency and self-control are, well, not so hard to maintain, though hands tremble and eyes bulge and semen stains are as common as cola spills. Paul interviews "Miss 19" and she can't name a single province in Iraq or the Vice President or the year of the French Revolution, which is unfair and irrelevant since she can and does tell Paul you can't get AIDS just by hugging a person, and you can't not believe in God just because there's suffering in the world, like, say, Bangladesh. In the meantime, Charles is speaking not to his freckled lesbian nymph Catherine but to Elisabeth, a coy girl, a likeable girl, who leans against a wall outside the cinema and fiddles with the thin gold chain around her neck, sliding her fingers back and forth on it, as Charles imagines those fingers on his cock, though he maintains his demeanor and presses forward (as it were) with questions about her breasts, recalling how he reached for the sugar across a young woman in the café so that he could brush against her sweatered breasts, and Elisabeth is surprisingly forthcoming, describing the color and size of her nipples, when she first began wearing a bra, whether any man had ever touched her *naked* breasts (no), then reluctantly but without being asked, detailing how she shaves her pudendum, how she lubricates her vagina, how she sometimes can't stop rubbing down there while in the bath, until she throws back her head and moans. As she does now in front of Charles, whose erection is already at full mast. What can Elisabeth do but laugh? And laugh? Is this really the twenty-first century? The question that Paul must have had in mind as he was backing up on the terrace of the new apartment that he and the girl and Catherine have leased in a high-rise building on Second Avenue overlooking a Turkish restaurant where a beautiful young woman in a Cleopatra wig and short skirt stands on the sidewalk and motions people in. Yes, what time was he living in, he must have been thinking, as he held the digital camera chest high, the girl and Catherine nicely framed in the viewer, the girl now pregnant (and famous, her recording rising on the charts), though she hasn't told him yet, Catherine holding the girl's hand smiling as if in a real estate commercial, Paul inching back and for some reason suddenly sympathetic to his friend Charles's mutilated foot, remembering also the faces of his companions that were blown off in apparently secure neighborhoods, remembering the girl's hand on his back in the middle of the night, asking for more, Catherine next to her sound asleep, so that he wondered what they had been doing with each other while he'd been sleeping, causing him to look at the viewfinder again, Catherine's arm around the girl, as he leans against the railing on the terrace and flips over it and falls fourteen stories down, almost hitting the woman in the Cleopatra wig.

The Family
This time she is married with two children, she has long auburn or light brown hair, her accent slightly Russian as she says things like "We go to movies," and her husband's name is not Paul but Robert, though everyone wants to call him Roberto, and her blue-eyed gaze moves ever so slowly from object to object in the cramped apartment, their income mostly dependent on Robert(o)'s work as an auto mechanic in a shop he doesn't own, though later as she drops off her youngest child, a little girl always crying, at a kind of daycare center that takes its payment in goods like cans of fish or new pajamas or a gross of condoms, one discovers within minutes that she earns her own money through prostitution (which dates this entire episode but what can you do, the endless wars are bad enough, homes being lost in defaults, the collapse of credit, jobs lost, who cares what a stranger wants to do with her body, as long as he doesn't...?), but all that is delayed while she shops for a new coat and later meets a girlfriend at the café where she occasionally picks up clients, and as the camera swings from her chatting with the friend to a hotel room, her gaze quizzical, then amused, then, well, flat, bored, as she tells the not-much-more-than-adolescent boy he can't watch

her undress (where did he get all that money? Has he pinched the tuition for the private school he attends in Riverdale?) because that would be degrading, to allow him to see her shed the lovely garments her children are accustomed to seeing her in, though it might be a toss-up to believe that the issue is where she can place her folded clothes so they won't be soiled, whether her cellulite shows as she bends this way or that, whether in watching her step out of her skirt, remove her bra (breasts heavier and with more droop since the children), slide her panties off her hips, down her legs, bending as if to receive the boy that very moment, she just doesn't want him to be evaluating her as a product, which as everyone knows is what most of life is about — products, consumer confidence, consumer disappointment, consumer despair, consumer hunger, consumer afflatus, consumer satisfaction, though that is never possible because the world is always in motion, coming toward or going away, and need incessant, whereas to be still, to be content, is to be dead, whereas the woman is herself a copy of the world moving like a struck pinball *ka-chinging* her way through the hours that she is away from her husband and children, making, it is true, enough money to pay for the layaway coat in the store she was seen in before the first client of the day, though on her arrival home, with the little girl still crying at her side, and with Robert(o) having been speaking with a young girl in another of those cafés part confessional booths, part peeping tom stations (are we in Paris?), where he told the girl that she was pretty enough, though she never quite asked about that as she dredged herself for (something authentic, the meanings of life? love *[gasp]* ?) a sign or a voice that leaned into a future, and all Robert(o) had in mind was he wasn't interested in her body, having a beautiful woman at home, and here he is now, at home, not too interested in his wife's body after all, or in his son's homework, as the boy writes out a narrative of his adventures in what in another context someone might have called the skin trade, except that title was long ago used by a Welsh poet, and the boy's mother, looking over his shoulder, is thinking exactly that, *Adventures in the Skin Trade*, remembering her own day, her product placement, her handful of crisp new bills, as she sadly reheats last night's dinner while her husband crouches toward the TV and CNN's *Situation Room*, the boy writing his next sentence in a spiral notebook, his little sister crying while her mother suddenly recalls Moscow, her father's vodka-laden breath, his hands on her young hips, her mother in the bathroom with an ice pack on her eye, the snow falling and falling, the small paring knife in her hand, the at-first-bloodless seam she makes on her father's neck, the eventual but slow spill down onto his shirt collar, then under his shirt, his head flung back, his eyes turned to heaven like a stricken saint's, her mother screaming but secretly relieved, secretly happy, secretly vowing to throw her daughter out, which she does once the father is in the hospital, when an uncle gets her a visa, when she comes to Brooklyn, when she goes to high school with cousins, when she sleeps with and marries the mechanic who fixes her uncle's car, then spends her days in an Astoria apartment near the Triborough Bridge trying not to watch soap operas, not always being with children once they can talk, not sitting next to her husband in the evening as he follows the war(s) news and the faces that flash silently on the screen of the newly dead when she herself is trying to not be shown there herself.

DEAR SIS...

MONICA, THE WOMAN in the cell with me, just laughed when I told her I took the plea bargain. "Honey," she said, "it ain't gonna be any better anyway, not if you're going to the joint. We can't not be who we are and that's the problem, ain't it?" But they're giving me a couple of days, before I get sentenced. I wish I was like everyone else, on the boardwalk, going past Indiana Avenue and smelling hot dogs and raw clams. *I'll have to break the lease on my apartment in Jackson Heights. But the personal things... I'm sending you the keys. Take anything you want and give the rest to the Salvation Army. Beth is three? What have I been doing while you had two daughters?*

And to think I came here to forget my crappy job. All I needed was Atlantic City and the sun and the boardwalk. I had a new Roxanne blouse, shorts, sandals, a great sun hat. I figured if I meet someone, fine. I mean, it's 1971. Anything can happen. The motel is right on the boardwalk, with an indoor pool. And terraces. And a lounge. I feel like one of those bees in Yankee Stadium, when the Jehovah's Witnesses had their meeting, those bees swarming over thousands of plastic plants and phony yellow flowers and getting nowhere and getting angry and bunching up like tourists at a blocked exit at an airport. At third base there were two swimming pools where everyone got baptized. I don't know what's worse, being one of the bees or one of the Christians, buzzing around a fake chrysanthemum or being drowned in someone else's ideas. What can you trust? Look at the man in Westchester who died from botulism in a can of vichyssoise. One paper says only 2% of our soldiers returning from Nam are addicted to heroin. Another says it's 4.5%. A Satan cult in Vineland is tying dolls stuck with Voodoo pins to trees. Louis Armstrong is dead.

I expected Joshua to be someone I could sort of want or not. Look at how it all started. Just think when ... (*Just a minute. There's something. I feel like I'm thinning out. I'm not real anymore. Not real. Real.*) Okay. It's okay now. (*It's like you can't see me until you connect the dots. A pencil-point scratching down my side. Somebody drawing me. Maybe that's why I stayed with him after I saw his explosives — to blow away the hand that was making me.*)

I met Joshua on the second day. We sat in the sauna, then we ran and jumped in the pool — I wore the two-piece Elizabeth Stewart I'd bought for the trip to Puerto Rico. *Remember*? When I think about it now, I could laugh. I almost laughed in his face when I caught him staring at me. I was climbing out of the pool. We went back into the sauna and I let my sinuses dry out. *You know how they've been since Mama died.* He was telling me he was a lawyer, he might get a job with the Department of the Interior. He said it was a chance for him to get into politics. I almost fell off the bench, laughing, right there in the sauna house, with both of us sweating and a little fat man outside, rubbing the window, looking in *(the way Mama would look into the car and count heads before we went to Palisades Park, and Richard would be telling you and me to cut it out because he had a headache and we were jumping up and down, and he'd be brooding, picking at his nails because who needs to go on rides with baby sisters?).* It was very airless.

I hope I can breathe where they send me. I could be like the Apollo astronauts, wearing a bubble on my head, digging for rocks in the moon's crust:

> If I can lean down.
> That stuff is really soft.
> Help me get it with the scoop. Atta boy.
> I'll throw it up, you catch it.
> Easy does it.
> Okay, let me get down here. Let me use my
>   tongs to pick it up.
> Hold it right there. Up a little more.
> I got it.

I can't help thinking of Monica, the woman in jail, on her cot, laughing, saying, "That man was no good at all! He left me behind like a sack of bricks." They'd been stealing a car on Ventnor Avenue, and her boyfriend Izzy was shaking all over he needed a fix so bad. He just drove off and left her there when the owner of the car came out and grabbed her. They found the car smashed into a pylon in Longport. I thought, that's what Joshua did, just left me. But there's not enough of him left to put in jail.

There I was laughing at him, seeing how his hair was combed to one side because he was getting bald, him behind his John Lennon glasses, always kind of sucking in air just before he made a fist and jabbed at you with something like, "People are basically selfish." I wondered, why is this guy hanging around in Atlantic City? His convention (what a laugh) was not being held in the big center where they have the Miss America pageant, where outside on the boardwalk there's a row of Greek columns, and a couple of months from now Miss Congeniality and Miss-I-Screwed-the-Judge will pose in the wind, hair blowing across their mouths, their legs squeezed shut like virgins.. Right now it's just men going past pushing people in wicker roller-chairs. There are striped cabanas in neat rows on the beach and a lot of fat people from Philadelphia waddling down the slat-walk in the sand. The tide is pulling out. On the Million Dollar Pier you can see the needle tower with the doughnut car that slides up and down, up and down.

The Ice Capades were in the center where the Olympic medal winners stick out their rear-ends and scrape past you in red-white-and-blue. Joshua took me. He took me to the ice show. He thought that was where he'd put the bomb, though I didn't know that. I was thinking, how can this guy, being friendly and harmless with me in the sauna, ever get into politics? You can see right through him. I figured, okay, he's selling himself as a big shot. He's probably a salesman. But I was up for it. I wanted a little fun. When I asked him if he'd been in Nam, he said no. His brother was. Killed by a booby trip in a Vietcong tunnel. Dead—for a lot of peasants. He screwed up his face and you could see he wanted to spit.

I shut up and thought of Richard dying in Korea.

The students last year shot by the Ohio National Guard.

I looked into the souvenir shops along the boardwalk, the antique clocks in the windows, and they stared out at us, the ivory fat-belly gods, demons with weird faces and twisted mouths. ("Bye, honey," Monica said. She leaned against the bars, on the outside, and grinned crazily at me. "Don't let the bedbugs bite. Ha, ha!" *Her sister had bailed her out, the way I know you would have, if I had asked you. But then, they remanded me without bail. Stupid. I mean it's not like I killed anyone.)* You could smell clams and hot dogs and taffy and pizza, while somewhere our soldiers were getting their legs blown off, and all these people from Montréal strolled past, pale from years of no sun, speaking French.

I knew if Richard had been our age, he'd have been in this war instead of the other one. But he would've been killed in this one, too. Then I think, look: the Selective Service just had their drawing for men born in 1952,

*the year Richard was killed. But 1952 was a leap year,
so they have 366 birth dates to give numbers to, for the
draft lottery numbers for 1972. What if Richard had been
killed on the extra day? What if it had been 1953 and that
extra day didn't exist?*

They might as well give me the chair.

In Denver in five days they had thirty-six fire
bombings and two dynamite blasts. I don't know where
Joshua gets off, talking about politics like it was just a
job.

We had dinner at the Traymore Hotel. I asked
him what about the convention and he just shrugged.
I wondered if he was just a vacuum cleaner salesman
talking himself up. His eyes never had hardness in
them but they looked away a lot. Once in a while, he
jerked his head to the side and blinked. A real tic. So
what? I thought. I could see he liked expensive places,
with headwaiters.

Later, we went to the Steel Pier. But why go to the
Traymore, this fake Arabic hotel, white and huge and
old, with arches and tile mosaics in curved ceilings,
why go there and then follow Joe Everybody in his
wrinkled clothes to the arcades? Joshua was holding
my hand and putting his arm around me in the crowds
and telling me how good my hair smelled. Oh, brother!

We saw Cab Calloway and the Kane Sisters — and
I thought which one of us, you or me, would get the
straight lines and who the *yuks* if we were up there
wearing black taffeta and showing our polished teeth
and talking it up before we held each other around
the waist and sang up there on that slanted stage.

(As if Mama would ever have let us do that, ever been fooled by those talent scouts who came around the neighborhood.) Calloway led the audience in his song and Joshua was shouting at the top of his lungs, *Hidee-ho, hidee-ho, hiddee, hiddee, hiddee.*

I could see Joshua was into it, into screaming in an old theater with dusty drapes on the walls and broken-spring seats with bald velvet backs. Everywhere you could smell wet socks, crotches, sand, mildew, the dope in people's hair. I could see something wild and violent in him, which you wouldn't expect because he always talked so low, explaining things like some nutty teacher. Or a shrink. *(When I saw Dr. Reister after Mama died, all he wanted was to give me pills. At first.)* But inside. Inside Joshua was this man who listened to all the lawyers' arguments, watched the stock market go up and down, who read about the underground tests in Amchitka, who heard the dykey woman marine captain talk about Alice America, the woman who doesn't exists, who joins up the way I was joining up and didn't know it. Inside Joshua is this man wearing glasses like Trotsky who I read about, his pig eyes hot, spit flying off the end of his little beard (inside himself he's grown a beard, he's yelling at crowds from a balcony), who thinks it's better if the world ends. Meantime, he's talking so low I can hardly hear him. He smiles, looking out at the sea, the dark hair on his forearms like little whirlpools. I saw a girl with legs like mine, like rails. *I remember how Daddy slapped me the first time he caught me wearing make-up.*

That night, after I found out about Joshua, what he was up to — what I *thought* he was up to — we went to the end of the pier to see the circus acts and the diving horse. He kissed me, hugged me. We sat on benches built out over the ocean and I got so nervous I waited for all of us to fall into the surf, the circus people swinging on their trapeze way above the nets, somersaulting. Joshua bug-eyed. I thought, I bet acrobats are never bored. One slip, you're dead. The diving-horse was a real horse, but he only slid down this tilted platform and fell into a tank of water.

Remember how Mama told us about love, how we thought it was great only because we wanted it that way, to be wonderful? If she had been here, she would've said, "But after the horse slides into the water, how does he get out?" And Dr. Reister with his hand on my knee telling me I had great hair and I told him it ran in the family, and he said, "There's just one more thing we need to do," moving his hand along, as if my mind was between my legs. But Mama couldn't know. Mama was dead... When gelignite goes off, the horse flies up into the air, goes way up in the air and comes falling back like something biblical, a horse falling from the sky, splashing down, even though you're used to reading about the astronauts doing that, and this horse is like the red one falling off the Mobil sign, bleeding, floating, sinking. And bits of Joshua everywhere.

Once I asked him what color hair his wife had. "Almost black, like yours." And eyes? "Brown. Like yours." (*I think maybe in prison there'll be a counselor and we'll talk about the future, like in that movie 2001. Maybe*

I'll be working in a factory along a river somewhere. I imagine this Oriental woman, this planner, dressed like a warrior, with thongs crisscrossing her breasts. She has little beeping lights set into the rims of her ears. She tells me, "We can't change your race or anything like that." "What time are you from, originally?" I ask her. "Me?" Some of the lights twinkle and beep in her ears. "In the when I come from the sun is beginning to swell." "Is the world ending?" I ask. "Didn't you think it would?" she replies.)

I remember Mama just staring at the wall all that year after the divorce. I thought of it when Joshua told me about his marriage and he said he was a responsible person, he had a lot of insurance, no one would ever starve on his account. He didn't tell me yet his wife had taken a lover. And he himself was taking this vacation, while his kids were with his mother. He leaned towards me and kind of hissed, making a fist, then dropped his hands, went limp, looked away.

I thought of the children in Korea that Richard used to write home about. I remember the day Eva Perón died in Argentina, the day that King Farouk abdicated in Egypt, and a woman was blown out of a plane at 12,000 feet when a door opened behind her and she was swept out, while her husband was next to her smoking a cigarette. The same day the enemy was attacking Richard's aid station near Old Baldy, west of Chorwon. I remember going back to the Times *for that day, where they always carried the war news on p. 2. I remember them saying the enemy artillery and mortars fired 6,510 rounds — 2,317 more than the day before. (Me and numbers. Remember how I used to drive Mama crazy, telling her how many cars were waiting at the light, how many mints were in a box?) If there had been one less round that day, Richard's day, one less shell... It makes you feel so hopeless. Like hearing we'll be out of Nam in two years and then they give you the body counts. Or they tell you about this peasant and his wife working a rice paddy, how they return to their little house where they step on a mine. You see them burned into charcoal and kicked to the side of the road.*

I cried when Joshua told me his story, the way his wife had left him. We walked towards Ventnor, the moon big enough to fall out of the sky and the tide crashing. I felt like someone in a novel. Like Joshua was Lord Rochester and I was Jane Eyre (*remember Orson Welles as Rochester, his big eyes? That voice, oh, that voice...*) consoling him. I almost felt like that girl in the French movie *My Life to Live*, which I saw on the worst date in my life, though its real title was *Vivre sa vie* (*you think I forgot all my high school French*?) and all my date cared about was that she was a prostitute, but she wasn't really. Not deep down. She just wanted a life.

Joshua and I went to a female impersonator show, "The Queens Are Wild," at Fat Jack's. They looked better than me, those men, with their make-up and falsies and black-net stockings, and boas, and tight asses. Joshua didn't think it was so cute, so we left. I started to wonder about lawyers having conventions and about me staying another couple of days. Who's going to miss me at the plant, in an office that smells of raw sugar piled in burlap sacks on the dock, all those workers in white shirts and white pants keeping themselves sterile as surgeons while they mix syrup in tanks big enough to float a ship, and pump it all toward the machines that fizz carbonated water and syrup into bottles spinning around on carousels? Joshua can't be a lawyer. Maybe he's not even married. (*It's now. I don't know what's coming, what's happening. I feel like I'm coming apart. Can you read this? Am I writing this?*) We were wrestling on the bed in my room, and I forced him down. I said maybe he should've been in the show at Fat Jack's. But he didn't laugh. His face turned red, and he was sweating, and he was really pissed. I almost laughed. MAN DEFEATED IN LA CONCHA MOTEL.

Then I found his black bag. The explosives. The detonators. I realized the quietness in him was like this stuff waiting to go off. And I never knew what I was looking at. *Maybe when he frowned and threw up his hands, I should have said Richard died a long time ago in a different war and I'd forgotten about all that, how he got screwed when guys like you years later have a wife and kids and a good job. Maybe I shouldn't have thought doing something now was for that time, for Richard's dying. Maybe I should have known that all these years it was festering in me and I was bitter that Richard's war in Korea just didn't count. It was like it never happened.* Everything was Nam. In your eyes, up your nose. The dead-meat smell of bodies in ditches at My Lai. (I really want to be writing this in the Submarine Bar at the Traymore that is having a Boardwalk Bonanza plan. I hear they're going to blow the whole place up soon, to build casinos. Joshua could have saved them the trouble.

I'm fading again. But let me finish. I'm almost done. My hair is a mess. I imagine this handsome busboy with white teeth and long legs. He probably won't have his draft number picked for another year. They won't touch him. The way he smiles at me. He's leaving a note under my saucer with his name and the motel and everything on it. Maybe where they send me there'll be a river and I'll think I'm looking down at the Seine, I'm in Paris.)

Joshua wouldn't've lost his wife if she hadn't been so spoiled, so used to everything, waking up one day and blaming Joshua because he'd given her a home and a safe place. She gets a conscience. I can see her meeting a vet at some rally. He's got a drug habit but he touches her heart (never mind her pants) because he's angry and hurt, while Joshua (a car salesman? insurance?) is a man who always seems hurt somewhere but he won't tell you he's angry. Or feeling anything. And for some reason he can't talk about his brother. But this quietness in him is just a way of controlling everything. He won't tell about Trotsky inside him. He's visiting the kids' teachers, which his wife is not doing because she's feeling everybody's too privileged, and something has gone rancid inside her, something that wants to get out from under Joshua's voice and his eyes. She gets involved with this Nam vet. She gets pure. She's lucky no one asks her to stick up a bank, a rifle hanging from her shoulder, a beret pulled down over one eye. She's lucky she doesn't get blown up herself, making bombs in a little house in Greenwich Village. You know this bitch is going to have a movie made from her life because she's going to write a book about finding herself.

After learning about his wife, Joshua starts to mope. His customers thin out (clients, defendants, customers, what's the difference?) because everyone sees he's not into things. He buys one of those radical journals that have diagrams and instructions for a bomb. He puts on some raggy clothes and goes down to East 10th Street and buys the stuff. Probably from his wife's boyfriend without even knowing it. And he's here, with me, proving that he can do this. Maybe he thinks his wife will come back to him. You just want to stop people having fun, he says. You just want to stop all this forgetting about what's important. I don't know that on our visit to the Steel Pier, just as the diving-horse begins his slide toward the water, Joshua's going to stand up in the crowd, waving the detonator over his head, yelling.

(Now I'm wondering, what if he hadn't given us time to get away from him, time for me to run into the roofed part of the pier, and turn around to see the whole thing go off, Joshua, the platform with the horse, the horse, a couple of workers, everything blown up in the air, out to sea, people screaming everywhere, hot air blowing air into the pier, almost tearing my clothes off, all kinds of stuff flying around us. I don't know why I wasn't hurt. I mean, really injured.)

I think about that busboy at the Traymore who would have left a note for me under the saucer he didn't take away. How he'll treat me like a gift when I show up at his motel, not like the cops who found me, and how did they do that anyway? He'll be going down on me, licking his way into me like I'm his older sister he's been watching for years through the keyhole in the bathroom door, while I'm flipping through *The New Yorker,* looking at the cartoons (*If someone connects all the dots and I'm visible again, will you visit?*), the jokes about wives leaning over their husbands with some kind of letter in their hands (*Don't bring the kids. Their convict aunt. What next? Peace in our time?*), accusing them of buying the wrong dog food, the kind of crap that marriage gets to be about... don't make me laugh.

I have to stop now. I have to go.

HIS STORY

THE DIRT ROAD ran along a rain-swollen pond, then veered to the right, toward a paved road with the same name as the famous ape laboratory, Yerkes. That road emptied onto Route 138, which took David Burns past the local firehouse, the small auto shop that had just serviced his Avalon, and the shopping center with the A&P that until last year was neighbored by Forum Video, where once or twice a week he used to rent something from the X-rated rack in the curtained room at the rear. "I should be enough for you," his wife Roxanne said, once walking in on him while he sat, Bushmills in hand. "You are, my dear, you are," he said, pressing the STOP button on his remote and switching to the evening news. But the video store was gone and now he accessed erotic sites on the Internet, floundering in ads for online sex, treatments for erectile dysfunction, real-time cams from sorority dorms, and when Roxanne used the computer, working each day on her novel, going later to email one of her daughters, she found all kinds of lurid invitations. "I wish you'd keep your shit off here," she said. It was her own fault for not getting a separate e-mail address. But it was a way of keeping tabs on him, to see if he was still in touch with Morna Tor. That had been their deal — she'd retire with him to this bucolic corner of North Salem, if he'd give up his girlfriend.

David knew that Roxanne was writing about him and Morna. He wondered if her petulance and the increasing croak of her voice were part of the story. If she'd made him a prick. She kept everything on a diskette that she removed each day and he knew where she probably hid it. Among her mother's jewelry. Or slipped between the covers of the baby books she'd kept on her children, with locks of hair curled into pockets on the page. Or among the letters she kept from friends. It was a matter of honor not to snoop into her things. Not to expose his need, even to himself, his curiosity, his desire for a final encomium after all the others had faded into echoes of the farewell dinners, the people on stage saluting him as the only president they'd ever care about, the certificates of merit ("As if I was in junior high!" he'd mocked), the letters from old students and colleagues. He was as proud of his self-control as he was of always being the tallest man in the room. At six foot eight, with an almost elfin face and sardonic grin, his charm as he bent toward his listener was the product of surviving a stressful childhood, the war in Europe, a mediocre publishing record, years of bureaucracy, a parsimonious board of trustees — and years of impotence, which he had accepted until he hired Morna to head the Romance Languages department, from the first moment entranced by her swaying dark hair, her giving and forgiving smile, her silky voice that seemed in immediate contact with his loneliness that had never before been such a physical thing, a voice that when directed to other people had the muscular twang of a struck tennis racket.

HE CAME UPON them as he was organizing the garbage under the sink into a plastic bag. Three pages! She must have printed something out to proof — she hated reading text on the computer screen. The pages, crumpled and tea stained and clotted with bits of mango, had bypassed the usual pile of office paper recyclables that he took to the dump once a week. Roxanne's dramatis personae and the original people they were based on immediately obvious:

> Lester Goldstein, a college president, tall, casual in his authority
> His wife, Arianne, a thin red-head, an artist, her beauty fading
> Vivian Dale, Chair of Romance Languages, always leaning toward her listener, false sympathy in her voice

David stopped and thought back. *Roxanne had been such a lovely woman, small and red-haired, with* astonishingly white skin, perfectly shaped legs, a melodic lilt to everything she said as if always at her piano, as if never having been married, never having two children, her parents watching them while she and David went to a motel.

Now, in these pages, Arianne, Roxanne's clone, comes upon Lester, David's double, and Vivian Dale, a slightly thicker version of Morna Tor.

Arianne can almost see Lester's handprint fading on Vivian's bare knee.

He stands, smiling in a tired, noncommittal way, not caring anymore what anyone thinks.

David hadn't been able to tell Roxanne how beautiful she was, that the blood and wreckage of bodies on Omaha Beach still existed somewhere below his consciousness, though never quite in his dreams any longer, just always there, like a wet slippery surface below fallen leaves, and he knew if he stepped forth he would slip and topple.

Arianne asks if Vivian would like to join them on their holiday in Maine.

Lester is saying no, it's not a good idea. They'll be going from place to place up there. It wouldn't be any kind of hospitality for a friend. She'd be virtually alone.

"I could manage that!" Vivian says brightly, crinkly from too much sun on the tennis court, somewhat hippy from bearing three children. She holds her hands aloft as if to smooth an invisible fabric, or with her spread fingers to frame Arianne's paintings that adorn the spacious college-owned house in Riverdale.

Arianne recognizes in Vivian an energy she used to have.

The third page ends with a stain over *vivacious*, as Vivian is now walking around the room, commenting on Arianne's work, calling it *authentic* and *inspired*.

He and Roxanne and Morna had all gone to Maine, where Roxanne, boozed to the hilt, almost drowned herself. Lester Goldstein. Couldn't she have gotten a better name?

Whether or not the almost daily, squeezed-up, discarded pages were something Roxanne intended him to discover, he couldn't say. If she meant him to find them, he was happy to play the game. She was beginning to trust him again. If not, he had the right to see if she was making him ludicrous, ridiculing his inadequacies — he, a man known as a war hero, who had before that already survived changing his name from Bernstein to Burns (which never prevented the three-Manhattans Roxanne from calling him a Jew bastard every Christmas, and kissing him), a man who had forced the closure of several academic departments to form divisions with division heads, appointing new chairpersons of departments, a man so charming, so image effective, he hosted a weekly show in the arts on local public TV. A man whose right hand now trembled as he brought a spoon to his lips. Who occasionally discovered he'd been incontinent. Who haunted the Internet dreaming that Morna would find a way to communicate with him from the fastness of the Midwest college where she was now chancellor.

"IT'S WORSE THAN ever," Roxanne complained, holding her hand to her throat. It was unclear when her voice had begun to fade. He would speculate it was a form of self-punishment in a woman who still believed she'd not done enough for her children, both of whom she sent — half to one, half to the other — the proceeds of her Social Security check, not to mention the checks she insisted he write to bail out her grandchildren. It was just before he retired that a verbal apraxia had seized one of her vocal cords and her voice became a weepy, whispering thing. He blamed the years of smoking. An intern had suggested the long-delayed influence of being exposed to her sister Rachel's bulbar polio when they were children, when Rachel died. Now the doctor was calling it abductor spasmodic dysphonia and every five months he injected Roxanne's larynx with botulinum toxin, which made her tongue unwieldy and for several days her voice a baritone. Her daughters laughed when they heard her on the telephone. He would grimace and try to bury himself in the Mets game being televised. But the toxin always wore off and Roxanne would cry when he shouted that he couldn't understand her. She wrote more furiously than ever. And he upbraided himself for his impatience, though things would explode out of him without warning, as if he were back in the presidential chair scolding a wayward faculty member. He dreaded what he might find on the pages tossed into the trash that day.

But he was grateful that she hadn't gone into anything clinical about impotence. Arianne's husband Lester remained fully capable, which made his betrayals more poignant. It wasn't that Vivian Dale, Morna's representation in the novel, could rouse him like no other woman, his wife or the secretaries or the women he'd meet in conferences. He slept with all of them, almost in equal numbers, bedding women as easily as taking out the trash or blowing his nose. There were days when David would almost become aroused as he pressed the balled-up pages flat and read of the women moaning with pleasure, suspecting even so that Roxanne was tormenting him, that she wrote these pages to arouse him, to accuse him, to punish him with satirical excess, providing in her pity of him a flickering scenario of never-ending virility that drained everything moral and sensible out of his being. What was he but an empty shell?

"You're entitled to have one of your own," Roxanne had said, her blue eyes gleaming with accomplishment, her sculpted face beginning to fill out, her small breasts larger each week whenever he cupped them. She had gotten pregnant almost immediately after they married. And when their son Edward was born in Geneva, New York, where David was teaching that spring, Roxanne brought him home to their small apartment and her two daughters whom David had already accepted as his responsibility, and everyone danced around the infant boy, who was not destined to see a third year. "Maybe I didn't give him enough antibodies," Roxanne said. "Maybe I didn't love him enough, maybe..." David put his long arm around her, pulling her to him, feeling the sorrow that was nonetheless already thinning into relief — there would be one less child to rear.

In the novel, Arianne's son Edward *in possession of his own name!* was studying piano at Juilliard, not always getting along with his father, while his mother would set up her easel in the music room whenever Edward was at home and practicing his *études*. Mother and son working at their separate arts — David was moved, reading, then placing each wrinkled page on the chair beside him. And, after all these years, he began to feel the grief of losing his son, once he saw in Roxanne's narrative what Edward might have become. He also began to worry again that Roxanne knew that he was reading these pages and was feeding them to him to torment him.

"WE NEED TO get to some theater," Roxanne said, her voice crackling with the phlegm she had such trouble coughing up. "You're right," David agreed, "let's go to the ballet!" His enthusiasm surprised them both. Last week, she'd fainted in the bathroom. He had found her on the tiled floor, amazed that she hadn't struck her head on the sink or the edge of the tub. The doctor shrugged after all the tests showed nothing. "Try not to bend over and stand up too quickly," he'd said. "Avoid caffeine." He didn't say stop smoking. Cut back on the Canadian Club. Stop trying to throw parties with a dwindling list of people being nice who no longer had anything to gain from David now that he was retired. Stop wearing yourself out writing a book that will never be published. Stop breathing, why don't you?

David leaned over and kissed her on the head. "We get along," he was in the habit of saying. "*Romeo and Juliet* at the New York State Theater," he said. "Tchaikovsky?" she asked. "Yes." "Too bad. I really prefer

Prokofiev. But what the hell." He preferred Tchaikovsky. Prokofiev gave him a headache, the way that symbolism and allegory did in literature. Roxanne, thinner than ever but now almost radiantly beautiful as she seemed all essence — in spite of her hair thinning, dyed red, narrow tracks of white scalp showing — her face a carefully shaped energy that mimicked corporeal form, luminous and strange, so that occasionally David would shiver to look at her. In these moments, something of the past awakened in him, he tried to hold her, aware that she gave off a reflected light, like a fragile Baccarat crystal flute he was afraid would snap off in his hands. "Good!" He reserved tickets online and said he would drive them down, though lately he'd been backing into other cars in parking lots and seemed slower than usual to hit the brakes. But he'd struggled through worse in the drinking days, when he'd dismiss the college driver and take the car himself to a rendezvous.

The next day, after Roxanne had dumped her wastebasket with its tea bags and peach pits and papers into the general garbage under the sink, she had lunch with David and retired to the little den to read as she always did. He dutifully put the dishes into the dishwasher, wiped the table, folded the dish towel neatly and draped it over the back of a kitchen chair. He pulled open the door of the sink cabinet and pawed through the mess in the big white plastic bag that lined the trash can and found her pages, today less torn and crumpled. Lester, Arianne and Vivian had gone to Maine together, using the same cabin along the lake that David and Roxanne used to rent every summer, surrounded by tall pines, with a nearby beaver dam, a dock, a canoe and a swimmers' float about a hundred feet from shore. There were only two or three other cabins on what was really a large pond ("They call them camps," he'd told Roxanne once, when she was trying to give directions to friends).

The water was too frigid for Lester *and for David!*, but Arianne and Vivian — both in dark, one-piece suits, wearing bathing caps, Vivian taller, more broad-shouldered, Arianne whiter, her legs perfectly tapered — dived off the dock, while Lester swung in a hammock, reading a P. D. James mystery *actually, it had been something by Ian Rankin, the Scottish crime writer, and only Roxanne had entered the water, while David read and Morna tried calling her daughter on a cell phone that had no reception, and giving that up, she sat on the lawn chair next to him, her hand on his bare leg...*

The women swam to the float and pulled themselves up the ladder, laughing, neither of them feeling the effects of drinking white wine. *Roxanne had downed three Rob Roys and gone beyond the float, almost to the opposite shore, and begun gulping water, just as Morna's fingers were in his pubic hair... .*

P. D. James was completing her description of the lonely seaside where a body would be found, when Lester fell asleep. Arianne and Vivian swam back to the dock, where they stood for a few minutes, letting water drain off them. It was obvious how strong, even a bit heavy in the body, Vivian was. Her thighs showed ripples of cellulite that were nowhere to be seen in Arianne, who remained lithe, and if not girlish, athletic. The women took themselves inside the cabin, chatting merrily, the narrative flashing back to the time when Arianne had for many evenings consoled Vivian when her marriage dissolved. *Roxanne had done that with Morna. Why? Why?* Lester snoozed his way through what was left of the afternoon, guiltless and irrelevant, while Arianne and Vivian were stripping off their suits on the back patio and taking an outdoor shower together.

It was in the guest room that they began touching each other, Vivian's suitcase, in which she had brought the latest minutes of the faculty meeting, pushed to one side. Arianne had never imagined what inserting her tongue in another woman's mouth would be like, while Vivian explored her body with a practiced hand, then moving down, glided her lips up Arianne's thigh, around and into the crack of her buttocks, into her sparsely-haired V, finding her clitoris with a greedy tongue...

He got so excited reading he had to sit down — though his hope of an erection was unrealized. Was it possible that all those angers from Roxanne about his time with Morna were tantrums of jealousy not over him but Morna? But if she knew he was reading these pages...? He remembered how often Morna would protest that she loved Roxanne, even as she lay naked on her couch and allowed him to run his hand over her breasts and belly, down into her vagina, where his fingers found her moist and ready, while he muttered, "My god, I wish I could get in there." "Don't think about that," Morna told him, writhing with pleasure, grunting, moving her hips up and down, finally gasping.

David read the last of the day's pages, this one with a tea stain running down the middle like an uncauterized wound. Arianne, back home in her studio, was working on a new painting that Lester came upon by accident as he was looking for the *Times* that Arianne so often took with her to do the crossword puzzle. As was his habit when alone in the studio, Lester lifted the white sheet that covered Arianne's work in progress, expecting the usual river scenes or portraits of her friends. What he found was a drawing, half-worked in with bright acrylics, of an odalisque on the couch he recognized from the rented cabin, the same brightly colored bedspread used as a throw, the same chipped claw feet, the same indented cushions. It was Vivian, on her side, peering over her shoulder, the slope of her buttocks elongated, her expression one of amusement. The only item of clothing was a ribbon around her throat like an old-fashioned choker, a ribbon that Lester had seen around the gift Vivian had brought for Arianne when she arrived at the cabin. Inside the box had been a pair of long slender, handcrafted earrings that seemed more thread than metal. Almost gossamer. Arianne had cried out with delight.

DAVID DROVE WITH Roxanne into the city to Lincoln Center that Tuesday evening. She'd had a Botox injection two days before, so her voice was thick and deep, an effect that would wear off by the weekend. Her lean face showed fatigue. Her red hair seemed almost brittle. But she was as trim as a model in her form-fitted lavender suit, her long fingers that had been so agile over piano keys — even more so now over a computer keyboard — closed on the small glittering purse she used on such occasions. "We need to write a check for Deborah," she said, referring to her oldest daughter who was pregnant with a fourth child. Deborah scraped along as an elementary school teacher in Wilmington, North Carolina, where her second husband regularly lost his job, no matter what it was. "Haven't you people ever heard of birth control?" David responded. A test showed that Deborah's child was a girl. Roxanne twisted around in her seatbelt to stare at him. "You think she got pregnant by herself in some kind of parthenogenesis?" Her voice was scratchy and hoarse. "Wham, bam, thank you, ma'am," she said. "Then it's off to the pub." "The bar, the bar," he said irritably, disliking her little anglophilisms, her habit of quoting the Bard, often saying, "like Hotspur, 'I need employment,'" or worse, making fun of him, David, in public after she'd had a few, as when he had trouble fitting himself into one of the narrow seats in the student theater, to see a student play, and he sat next to her, and she teased, "Need to sit next to your mommy?" staring up at his elongated bulk, his scowl, and he glanced piteously at Morna who was sitting at the end of the row, hands in her lap, smiling encouragement.

It was the same thing that happened at parties, everything going fine, until the third or fourth drink, and Roxanne would slur, lean toward her listeners, fling out her arms, sometimes whisper, "You know what I do, what my vocation really is? I screw!" Where was the attentive young woman he'd courted, who smoked but declined spirits, who sipped ginger ale or white wine, who gave up a Ph.D. to follow him with her children to God knows where he might be going? "You know, mother never drank much, until she met you," Deborah accused during one Christmas holiday. "I never twisted her arm," he retaliated. "No, you didn't. You just got grumpy and withdrawn, and mother started doing what she thought you wanted, to keep you company, to take on your habits, because that's the way she is. She's such an empath." "Christ!" he said. And added, sneering, "You know, you shouldn't talk to your money tree that way." "Fuck you, David." Deborah, a woman like her mother, small but with a quick tongue and bad taste in men, spun around and joined another group, which happened to include Morna, who had, in her way, been courting both of Roxanne's daughters to show how sympathetic she was to Roxanne's difficulties in loving these adult women who seemed barely able to support themselves, while their mother played the role of the president's spouse, not to mention writing her stories and poems and getting regular rejections from *The New Yorker.*

But Roxanne wrote wonderful rhymed send-offs to anyone leaving the college group, anyone moving on or retiring, her narrative poems like something out of Alexander Pope, making David proud, though he wondered what it would be like if she turned her rhymes on him. "Oh, I like making it happen for others now," he said once to an old friend, who'd asked him if he continued to do scholarly work. "Like seeing Roxanne do what she does. She's a better writer than I could ever be." It had seemed a bargain — Roxanne playing his hostess, arranging guest lists, dressing beautifully, her long legs a wonder among women, her blue eyes flashing, all so that she could have her hours every day in her study writing, or playing the piano, though she'd gradually given up the baby grand in the music room, given up the little recitals she used to have with her friend Else at the cello in a spacious apartment near Columbia University.

"Deborah might not be having a good pregnancy," Roxanne said, touching his arm as he turned off the Westside Highway, toward the Lincoln Center parking garage. "And her husband's benefits are running out." "What about my benefits?" David said. "Christ!" But he always wrote the checks, because that was the deal, that was the basis of his honor, that was what Deborah referred to on another night, when she said, "Don't think I don't appreciate what you've done for all of us," referring to the years when her mother had brought two little girls and a broken marriage to her parents' frame house on Euclid Avenue in Syracuse, and David arrived one evening like a tall knight just out of his armor, grinning, the grit of war not yet cleansed from his hands that were reluctant to touch anything fragile. "How much?" he asked, turning into the garage. "How much do you have?" Roxanne teased. They both laughed. "Christ!" he said.

That evening, sitting in the First Tier, he held his hand on Roxanne's knee and enjoyed the improbable leaps of the male dancers, the ineffable grace of the prima ballerina, the swell of Tchaikovsky's music, and without wanting to or meaning to, he thought of Morna, wondered what she was doing on this cool fall evening, in some auditorium, no doubt sitting in the chancellor's chair, standing up to distribute awards, which is what happens to administrators — bestowing honors and prizes that would now be passing them by. And he wondered if he and Roxanne would attempt to make love when they got home, since he was writing a check, since he was now all hers. *Lester Goldstein would get laid...*

FOR SEVERAL DAYS, there were no pages in the trash. In the late afternoon, after Roxanne had finished with her writing, after they'd had lunch, David sat at the computer, his long legs bumping the keyboard, as he roamed the Internet, exploring the latest information on erectile dysfunction. The first doctor he'd ever consulted had asked, "Don't you find your wife attractive anymore?" David denied that, since there were occasions, like during their trip to Italy, when he was perfectly fine in bed. But it happened more and more, even if he had not been drinking and Roxanne hadn't become repellently inebriated, that his erections failed before they even started, and as patient as Roxanne was, she began to accuse him. "I'm sure you get it up with that tramp in the English office." Or, "Do I have to be twenty-eight all over again?" She tried everything she could, using oral stimulation, balms, fragrant oils she rubbed on his penis and his testicles, she even tried to talk dirty, to rouse his imagination before they got into bed. She watched pornographic videos with him, while he masturbated her, and she moaned convincingly, almost in harmony with the woman in the video. He was having trouble with other women as well, the one-nighters at conferences, the weekend retreats, the women who offered themselves because he was the president, because there might be something he could do for them — a job, a promotion, a recommendation. He'd been told about chronic tobacco use (he'd quit four years ago), diabetes, neurological impairment (well, his tremor was troublesome), pelvic surgery, pelvic trauma from riding a bicycle or a horse, prescription drugs, depression, vascular disease. The blood just didn't want to rise in the vessels that would swell his penis into attention. He was disgusted with the remedies doctors threw at him: intra-urethral pellets; oral drugs that caused backache, upset stomach, blurred vision; penile implants — balloons implanted in the penis, with a pump in the scrotum, a reservoir near the bladder; penile injections; a vacuum-creating cylinder over the penis that drew blood upwards, with a rubber ring at the base of the penis keeping the blood trapped, the penis erect. All of these solutions as if he were a problem in hydrophysics or a head case. It became widely known that he was impotent, in part because he confessed it to friends — who shrugged their shoulders in a there-but-for-the-grace-of-God-go-I — or because the fewer and fewer women he tried to bed began to gossip. But he was still the tallest man in the room. Grumpy at faculty meetings. Merciless with tenure-and-promotion decisions. Insistent when he disliked a program or wanted to bring one in. Increasingly seen as a dinosaur by the younger professors. An impediment. A situation that worsened as the older professors who had known him in his glory days retired. All of this reversed when Morna joined the faculty and reorganized Romance Languages, inaugurated a humanities program for the core curriculum, found a way to make him excited, at first because he found her so energized. and then because her hands and mouth on his body, though he did not achieve full erection, managed to get him to ejaculate.

That the influence of Morna was mental as well as physical, that it was something archetypal in her hold on him, became almost immediately obvious to Roxanne, who decided — it would seem — out of compassion for David, to make Morna a member of their intimate circle. It was surely better to see him happy than to worry about him being unfaithful. Though she'd for years accepted how he strayed ("You're nothing but an alley cat!"), there was never any permanence in his affairs. They were just the overflow of libido. The skimming off of excess sperm. It seemed more hygiene than anything serious. And she admitted to being somewhat relieved when he became impotent, in part because of her own declining interest in sex (with him, he thought), in part because he wouldn't be running around so much, making her the aggrieved, hapless, abandoned spouse, an image she constantly defied at parties, once she began to drink, by getting louder and more vulgar than anyone else. If Morna was known now as David's latest girlfriend, Roxanne could at least embrace her openly and frustrate public opinion. She was almost putting her imprimatur on the relationship — in her wisdom knowing that if she didn't, she'd lose him forever. And this is how David had come to understand their little unspoken arrangement, until he'd read the pages about Roxanne's characters Arianne and Vivian. It had never once occurred to him that Roxanne was herself drawn to Morna. Was it possible that she wasn't sharing him with Morna, but sharing Morna with him?

The next day, he found pages in the trash. There was a scene with Arianne's son, Edward. He was practicing at the baby grand in the music room, while his mother daubed at a water color of the tall, white and pink hibiscus in their backyard visible through the French doors *there hadn't been that kind of space and light in their music room*, and as the Chopin *étude* made its crystalline progress beneath Edward's adroit fingers described as long and pliant *like David's, when he was young, no arthritic bulges, no goddamn stiffness...*

Arianne commented on how beautiful it was, and her son nodded in agreement, even as he played. When he finished, and sighed, he asked, "Do you think Le Père will ever agree to Paris?" Tall, with his mother's eyes but his father's frown, he wanted his parents to accompany him on a tour that would end with a week playing in several distinguished private salons. "No, dear, I don't think so," Arianne responded. "He has too many things going on at the college." "And he needs you," Edward said almost mockingly, "so you have to stay here. " "That's right, dear." She completed the watery, parchment-like interior of a white hibiscus. "I hope you don't hate us." He was their only child. Arianne had married late and only once, after her mother died. "But you know, Vivian Dale is going. She's visiting her daughter" *which Morna did, only it was Montréal, at a conference on Romance Languages, and David went along. Roxanne was visiting grandchildren in North Carolina...*

Vivian herself walked into the room. "Taking my name in vain?" She kissed Edward on the cheek and did the same with Arianne, allowing her hand to linger on her waist. "Lester told me you were home," she said to Edward, "and I wanted to see you." Lester joined them, his height seeming such a burden that he was bent forward, as if carrying a weight behind his neck. A kind of ox. *Not fair!*

"I told Vivian she should have dinner with us tonight," Lester said. Arianne smiled. "Of course!" *how Roxanne would smile that smile, opposite Morna at table, and he never knew what she was thinking, never...* But that night, on the way home to his apartment in the Westside, on a rain-slick road, Edward could not prevent his car from sliding into a guardrail. His car sailed over it and struck a tree. When the police called, Lester was in his pajamas, holding a half-finished novel by Ruth Rendell, and Arianne had finished brushing her hair, turning half-frozen in her vanity chair, knowing a terrible event was unfolding.

David wondered why Roxanne was linking Morna, through the character Vivian, to their son's death so many years ago, until he realized that the death of the fictional Edward, the nascent concert pianist, was really the death of Roxanne's own relationship to music, which, like her writing, had altered forever after he and

Morna had returned from their conference in Montréal. It was the second nearly fatal wound to their marriage — the first being when she lost the real Edward to an absurd infection. But what had seemed so terrible to Roxanne about his return from that conference? Had it been his total lack of interest in even trying to make love? Was it his being resigned to their being married forever, though he was in a crucial way dead to her, and she knew that, but would never herself try to leave him, because... He couldn't even think the word *love*, it was so against his grain by now, but he did accept Roxanne's devotion to him as he had accepted his mother's care, that woman who in his childhood had insisted at the expense of his sister that he was special, even though his father was a failure at everything he attempted, down to transforming his name, shedding the "___stein," in the hope of moving up in the business world. Something in Roxanne was like his mother — seeing in him still something to admire, to respect, a strength, a goodness belied by his overt acts of unfaithfulness, not to mention the more damaging ones within, where he abjured her in his heart. "He's never really unhappy," he heard Roxanne say to Deborah on the phone. "He likes his comforts too much. His Bushmills, his chocolate-covered nuts, his grilled shrimp, his Mets and his *New York Times* and *Wall Street Journal*, his books on politics, his crime novels, his old movies. He never gets depressed about anything for very long." Then Roxanne was listening to whatever it was Deborah said. "No," she finally replied, "it's not narcissism. Or Asperger's. It's something else."

The next day, stepping off the back patio slate steps, Roxanne fell and fractured her hip. It wasn't a surprise to David, who had been observing something unsteady in Roxanne's gait over the past several weeks. He called 911, as she lay on her back. "I think I broke something," she said in not much more than a whisper, the benefits of the Botox injection having worn off. He tried to bend over and get her up, but it was too painful for her and too difficult for him, so he brought a pillow for her head and a blanket, watching her tilt her head back, grimacing, pale, so suddenly deathlike that he was terrified, his eyes filled with tears, he felt completely helpless. "You want me to read you something?" he offered. The rose of Sharon trees were still in bloom, their purple and white blossoms falling into the dewy grass, where they curled up, and the mild September air carried the scent of vegetable decay from the woods, though he detected in it a deeper, more pungent and nauseating sourness that he feared was a dead animal. "That's very sweet of you," Roxanne said. "You better sit down. You look awful." She tried to alter her position and grunted with pain. "Didn't you look where you were going?" he said, relieved that she seemed quite herself. "We're not all as balletic as you," she responded, knowing full well that his athleticism had deserted him in his late twenties, that his tennis playing had become a stationary act, as he waited for the ball to come to him and slammed it back or just let it bounce beyond his reach. He never moved much more that a few inches from his spot, in a kind of presidential prerogative that had others racing about.

"You better call Deborah and Madge." Both her daughters were planning to visit for her birthday in a couple of weeks. David dreaded the whole thing, the pregnant Deborah with her brood, her doltish husband, and Madge, divorced, her two kids, one of them a little strange. What would he do if they came now? "What should I tell them?" he asked, looking down at her. "Just bring the phone to me," she replied. Her pain was obvious, but so was her habit of organizing things. Deep creases appeared in her cheeks. Her voice cracked and receded and returned, losing its way, recovering — finding him, the way she had done for so many years, locating him in his retreats, bringing him back. "Does it hurt?" he finally asked. "Only when you ask me that."

David followed the ambulance to the Putnam Hospital Center in Carmel. He hated waiting rooms and nurse's stations, the latter reminding him of his days as a medic, and the smell, always the antiseptic — the sulfa he'd poured on wounds, gauze wet with blood, a man's eyes rolled back into his head, exposed viscera, a boy asking, "Am I dying? Am I going to die?" But he tamped all that memory down. This was Roxanne. She looked drained and frail in the room she shared with three other women, one of them moaning. She'd been X-rayed and interviewed, told not to move around too much, and given a painkiller. She reached a hand out to him. "Poor you," she said. "You better get some pizza for yourself. And one of those rotisserie chickens from A&P. And some bags of salad." "I'll manage," he said. He seemed quite stricken, but whether it was from grief or the inconvenience of not having her home was not clear, even to himself. She had called her daughters from her fallen position on the patio, before the ambulance came, Deborah expressing complete disbelief at what she was doing. "Are you mad? Where is David?" Madge, heavier in spirit than her sister, merely said, "Okay. But we're coming for your birthday anyway," making it seem twice as oppressive.

For the next few days, Roxanne became the darling of the nurses and the aides, learning their names, asking about their families, advising the younger ones on raising children, making them all laugh as she rolled her eyes when they asked about her husband. David would sit near the bed in an uncomfortable molded plastic chair, legs extruded, and read the *Times* or one of his books on baseball. Periodically, he would reach out and adjust her blanket or pour her some water or tell the nurse she needed the bedpan. One morning, walking down the hall to her room, he looked down and saw a circle of urine around the fly of his pants. He had wet himself and not realized it. "Christ!" He spent the day holding the newspaper in front of his crotch. Roxanne knew what had happened. "You can't help it," she offered. "It's because you're so upset."

Four or five days after Roxanne's fall, David received a letter from Morna. Somehow, the grapevine had conveyed to her what had happened (probably Roger Sykes, the PR man at the college, an ingratiating, untrustworthy man) and she was breaking their agreement because she knew that David must be in desperate trouble and she wanted to help. If only she weren't so far away. Her comments made him teary.

And he remembered the night she'd come to the house, when she told them that her husband had left her. Now David poured himself three fingers of Bushmills, added ice, and sipped slowly. He'd found something elegant in Morna, in her achievements (his own being limited to the editing of several textbooks), that excited him almost as much as the aura of availability that emanated from the firm, well-attired body of an attractive, middle-aged woman. But Roxanne had accepted her into their home, hadn't she? Was it entirely his fault? He was thrilled to read how Morna signed off in her letter.

I love you.

The days of visiting Roxanne in the hospital were filled with many small details. He brought her a lined pad and several pens, so that she could write down what she needed. Her voice had become extremely thin, and once, as she wrote out a request for her favorite perfume on her bureau at home, he complained, "I can't read your writing!" She wept quietly and rewrote her sentences, using bold, childish capitals, as a nurse's aide, a well-endowed black woman with a raspy voice, looked up and down by David, came in to take Roxanne's temperature and renew her drinking water. "How are you, sweetie?" Roxanne looked up and nodded, raising her left hand and making the OK sign with thumb and curled forefinger. "Just tell me if you need anything." She fluffed up Roxanne's pillows. Roxanne handed him the sheet of paper. On it, she'd written, ARE YOU EATING ENOUGH?

That same day, the doctor had taken David aside. "Look, your wife's hip is healing okay. But her voice— the neurologist was here. He says it's coming from her brain. The trouble is in the brain." It explained the periodic confusion she experienced trying to write out an idea, saying the same thing two or three times, or her sometimes blurry vision. She would, the doctor said, eventually lose her voice entirely. David kept it all to himself. He just couldn't stand it, watching Roxanne try to write something legible. He blamed her for not giving up smoking. He blamed her for not eating right, keeping herself so thin. He blamed her for being easily agitated. He blamed her for writing so much that got so little recognition that she'd ruined them both with her rancor and the smell of failure. I HOPE YOU'RE NOT JUST EATING MEAT she wrote. He said *no*, leaned over and kissed her on the head, and spent the rest of the afternoon reading in his plastic chair.

When he got home, he listened to the phone messages from Roxanne's daughters, and put a frozen TV dinner in the oven, his hand trembling. It was getting worse. A stress tremor, his doctor had said. It comes with age, sometimes. Nothing to do about it. Just be careful. You're really fine. But occasionally his hand danced up and down. Or he couldn't sign his name, as the pen swung back and forth. His left leg sometimes danced without warning, while he sat watching TV. But he managed. He was fine. He watched *The Asphalt Jungle* on Turner Classic Movies, and as the hapless girlfriend took the wounded hero into a meadow, he decided he would look for the diskette on which Roxanne had recorded her novel.

It wasn't hard to find. There, in a corner of the study, among the several magazines her work had appeared in, on top of her critical book about Edna St. Vincent Millay, sat a small brown envelope with "Heart's End" written on it. The label on the diskette within read "H's End," and was dated more than three years ago, with a dash. Which meant, he realized, that Roxanne had started the novel before he'd retired, before they'd moved here. He had no way to determine if the pages he'd been retrieving from the trash were recent or if they belonged to the time she began laying down the rules for their retirement, believing somehow that he was still capable of pursuing other women, that any woman would still find him — a tottering, ex-college president with no consultantship or political pull — attractive.

He calmed his hand that had been rising and falling as if he were bouncing a ball, and inserted the diskette into the computer. The contents showed twenty-four numbered chapters. He kept trying to match the events of the novel to the real ones that had inspired them. The plot seemed desultory, laden with descriptive details of Arianne's paintings, accounts of the parties that Arianne reluctantly hosted, though she was always elegant, welcoming, equipped with just the right vocabulary, hating things literary, as she tried to steer conversations toward art, but not ancient art, not the Greeks and Romans, not even Impressionism — "Their pictures are as blurry as their brains," she would say. Lester's presidency seemed to flow along in a period of not much political or social unrest. Indeed, the novel was more than a trifle dull, too aesthetic, David thought. Until Vivian Dale entered the scene, along with a thin, handsome and self-aggrandizing husband.

Reading that, David felt an "Aha!" rising to the surface. He sat back and thought of Morna Tor's husband, a belligerent, critical, accusatory man who couldn't wait to get a job away from her and New York. In the novel, at any rate, Lester Goldstein, tall and dour, hovered on the perimeter of a scene that excluded him. He may have been bedding numerous women, but none of them lightened his moods, and however one was to understand the bond between Arianne and Vivian, they both seemed happier for it.

Happiness. David leaned back from the computer screen. *Happiness.* An alien word, the expression of weakness, of need, of people who had never held a dying man in their arms or pressed their wet hands onto a hemorrhaging wound, trying to keep the sand out of it, trying to read the man's dog tags, trying to call his name above the thump of mortar shells. Yet, even as he thought this, he knew those experiences now belonged to something viewed on the History Channel, something recollected in meetings of the American Legion or the VFW, where men reminisced among themselves or for the annual interview with young reporters on Memorial Day, as their generation was slowly passing away. Which left him with what? With watching an aide change Roxanne's open-backed gown in the hospital, seeing how thin and bony Roxanne's lovely legs had become, seeing something opaque in her blue eyes when she looked at him, something turning away, sinking, though she kept trying to write out what she wanted him to do at the house, and he tried not to tell her he couldn't read what she was writing, because she would think he was ignoring her again, the way she thought he dissimulated poor hearing or kept silent because he utterly disagreed?

The phone rang. He felt a chill, fearing it was the hospital, but it was Roxanne's daughter, Deborah.

"Since mother can't speak on the phone, I have to ask you how she's doing." She sounded, as always, conflicted in talking to him at all. Somehow she blamed him, he knew, for her mother's accident. Even for her mother's voice problems. For the drinking. For the years of malaise underlying her mother's energetic routines. For the failure to publish well. For the death of their only son. For the breaking of a beautiful young woman's spirit.

Deborah continued. "I know you're doing what you can, but I think mother could be in a better facility." Burdened by her own husband and her own fertility, Deborah nonetheless, David understood, thought that she had to be on the job.

"Listen," he said, "she's going into rehab at a nursing home in Croton. Good people there." He didn't describe the old men left in the dayroom moaning in their wheelchairs, or the woman with hair straggling over her face, asking everyone who stepped off the elevator to take her home. Roxanne would be in her own private room, just outside the nurse's station, where patients with walkers scraped past all day long, and sometimes a foul odor drifted down the corridor.

"Well, I hope you're right," Deborah said. "It's driving me crazy that I can't get up there. But I can't." Her pregnancy was not going well. "Tell her all the children say hi and they love their Grammy."

"Okay," he said, "I'll do that."

"I hope you're taking care of yourself," she added.

"I manage," he replied.

After he hung up, he poured himself another Bushmills and took the TV dinner out of the oven. Crispy fried chicken with mashed potatoes, gravy, and string beans. He took the chicken piece by piece in his fingers, wiping his hands periodically on a napkin, until he'd eaten everything except the string beans. He sipped the Bushmills, took it and went back to the computer. He could see how the plot unfurled. The artist married to an academic administrator (who had published two books on Shakespeare), her work getting a show here and there but no major breakthroughs with critics, the husband's compulsive sexuality and indifference, the loss of their son. The appearance along the way of another woman, who at first seemed important to the renewal of the husband, when in fact she attaches herself to the wife, who in turn responds willingly. In the last chapter on the diskette, Arianne and Vivian say goodbye to Lester in the music room of his home, as they drive off to the airport for an exhibit of contemporary French painting in Paris. Lester is left standing at the piano tinkling a few meaningless notes.

With the text shimmering on the computer screen, David walked into the kitchen. Dispensed more ice from the refrigerator unit in the door. Returned to pour another Bushmills and scroll Roxanne's text back to the beginning.

Soon he would be tired enough to sleep.

THE QUEEN
OF HEARTS

STARTERS

A) Cucumber in Vinaigrette
Beth Romney had just begun sorting the candy hearts
for Valentine's Day in the cafeteria of a private school in
Atlanta, when her ex-brother-in-law Alan called to say
that Big Ed had died after two days on the respirator.

"Oh, no! How's Marjorie doing?"

"She's holding up." Alan described his mother's
state of grief over the past few weeks, but Beth drifted
away and began to worry how her daughter would take
the loss of her grandfather.

B) Cucumber Deep Fried

It was bad enough that the fourteen-year-old was still hostile over her mother's relationship with the art teacher, Edwin Phipps, whom Beth had stopped dating two months ago (not to mention her disapproval of Beth's current boyfriend).

"Why did Phipps ask so many questions? Why did you like a Negro so much?"

"That's not a word we use any longer," Beth replied. "It's 1995. Things have changed."

"Well, he is, isn't he?"

"Maybe three generations back," Beth said.

"You think race just wears off," Andrea snickered, "like shoe polish?"

"That's vulgar!" Beth scolded. "If it doesn't matter to me, why does it matter to you?"

"Because you didn't have friends every day asking you why your mother was dating a *Black* man!"

"He's not *Black!*"

C) Cheese Sticks

But only a few of Beth's suitors had seen the inside of her home, all of them eventually drifting away or being told by a Beth suddenly no longer vibrant, "It's not really working out, you know?" Which made her recent interest in Jamey Carlisle just another waste of time, according to her friend Stephanie: "You'll dump him like all the others. Honestly, I despair of you."

D) Sweet and Sour Shrimp
"There'll be a wake tonight," Alan said, quickly giving Beth the details. He had to get back to the elementary school where he was teaching. "Happy Valentine's Day," he almost snorted, and hung up.

E) Calamari (With or Without Breading)
While she was in her office, in the back of the food service area, trying to decide how to tell Andrea about her grandfather, Beth heard the workers Ky and Douglas having at each other. "You do what I say," Ky said — a small Vietnamese man, thin but energetic, often so concentrated on his tasks that he'd startle when spoken to. "You do it the right way. You do what I say." Douglas, nephew of the headmaster's secretary—she'd seen him come to work this morning, his lank hair pushed back over his shoulders, face puffy from a night of drinking and smoking — said, "There's more than one way to put on your pants in the morning. You can put in your left leg first. Or your right." Beth could hear Ky pacing back and forth near her door. "You do what I say. I tell you the right way!" Douglas sounded almost too bored to raise his voice. "What're you gonna tell me next. What side to part my hair on?" "You listen to me," Ky said. "I the boss!" "Oh, yeah?"

"Both of you stop it!" Beth shouted from her office. "We have hungry mouths to feed!" She was almost sorry she'd given Ky so much responsibility, not to mention hiring Ky's wife at the last minute. She had yielded to the look of sunken authority in his eyes, as well as his restaurant experience, for she knew that once, in that other country, his father had sent men to their death every day, that as a child Ky had watched his father, an ARVN colonel, bark commands to young orderlies, and here in Atlanta that man had been hardly distinguishable from the Chinese kitchen workers just smuggled in from New York.

F) Phone Snacks (Lo-salt)
Beth had just left a message for Jamey, telling him she couldn't make it tonight, when the phone she'd just clicked off rang alive.

"I suppose you heard about my father." Wayne sounded depressed — as usual.

"Yes," she said, "Alan called me."

"Did he tell you that he died alone? That no one was with him?"

"Oh, no, I'm so sorry."

"Yeah. He couldn't talk himself out of that one."

Big Ed had been Sales Manager for John Deere tractors, legendary among his peers, the kind of man who when asked not to smoke would blow smoke into the nonsmoking sections of restaurants, proclaiming, "I fought for my country!" After his coronary bypass surgery, he continued to light up his Camels. But to Beth he'd always been considerate, and when she divorced his son she told Big Ed and his jittery anorexic wife that they could see their only granddaughter, Andrea, as often as they'd like. He called Andrea "Squirt" or "Cute Stuff," and Beth had watched Wayne fade into gloomy silence in the high-decibel environment of his father, seen his drinking get worse.

"I'm so sorry, Wayne."

"Yeah. You gonna be at the wake?"

"Of course."

"And Andrea?"

"I haven't told her yet."

"Maybe she shouldn't go."

"Wayne, Big Ed was her grandfather!"

"Maybe she's too young for all of that."

Beth thought of Wayne's other daughter, the baby born to his second wife, with a hole in her heart, how Andrea had cried when she learned of the child's defect. "See, he's already broken *her* heart."

"She has to learn about these things," Beth insisted.

"You think everyone is like you?"

One of their old fights. Another had been his accusation that she always fell asleep while watching TV as a way of avoiding him. "I can't do this," she said, "I'm very busy."

"Yeah. Like I didn't know that." He hung up.

G) Letitia and Wanda (Grilled)

Letitia Johnson and Wanda Henderson were mixing nuts in with raisins for the love cups. Seeing them, after she wept in the ladies room for Big Ed dying alone, Beth thought Letitia actually seemed happy working side by side with the large and competent Wanda, who had lived in Germany (when her husband was stationed there) and who spoke German to Margaret the cake baker, so that Beth would say, " My kitchen is the U.N.," often looking to Wanda to keep a fragile peace. She recalled how Letitia would be in a huddle with several of the other women, some of them cleaning personnel, one of them saying, "Don't you let him. Just don't you let him!" Referring to Letitia's boyfriend, not to her ten-year-old son. Beth had almost felt empathy for the woman raising a ten-year-old boy by herself while also dating a problematic man, and she wondered if Letitia did things like letting her hair swing free over the food or leaving cartons open or the orange juice out too long to spite her or if it was because Ky, a foreigner, ran the kitchen, Letitia's look of blankness not incomprehension but disdain when Beth told her she'd have to wear a net over her dreadlocks. Not because they were dreadlocks but because everyone's hair had to be kept out of the food, offering no explanation for her own long, dark hair that swung free when she leaned over the soup, though she at least held a hand to her forehead.

H) Valentine's Day Tarts (Not Previously Frozen)
Sitting at her desk in the little office off the kitchen, Beth decided she'd have to tell Andrea later, perhaps call her out of class. She propped up the three Valentine's Day cards. One from her daughter — inside a large red heart it said, "You're the greatest Mom!" One from Jamey that had arrived in yesterday's mail, with a man and woman looking out to sea, saying, "It's not a real sunrise without you," which she found almost presumptuous for only three dates and one night of love making. The third valentine was printed as a queen of hearts playing card—"To Ms. Romney, From Her Staff," though Beth knew it was really from only Wanda. Is this what her romantic life had come to? Some evenings she'd slip

away to a bar with Stephanie, also divorced, also a member of Beth's gym, lean and attractive, and pretend to be available to the men who loitered, leaning over their drinks as the loud music engulfed them. Once, dancing at a club, with Stephanie wearing one of her goofy wide-brimmed red hats, Beth had given a false name to a man she liked the looks of, and invented a phone number, enjoying being pursued even if it was limited to one evening at a bar.

I) Phone Snacks (With Sweetener)
Jamey returned her call almost immediately. "I'd like to come to the wake," he said.

"But you never knew the man. Why would you want to see him laid out?"

"No, no, it's not that. I just want to be with you. I think I should be."

"But why?"

"For support."

"You think I'll fall apart?"

"No, no, no. This is the kind of time when you get to know who people really are."

"So this is about me getting to know more about you?"

"No, no. I mean I want you to understand I'm not the kind of guy who runs from unpleasantness. That's not who I am. I want to be there for you."

"Well, that's very sweet," she said. She thought of his card. The way in bed he continued to hold her after he came. How Wayne used to roll away from her. How this conversation was hemming her in. "I don't think it's a good idea. You won't know anyone there."

"I'll know you. And Andrea."

Who had said, "There's something *yucky* about him."

"Oh, Jamey, I'm really very busy."

"Of course, of course. Why don't I call you later?"

"Yes, yes. Goodbye."

"Goodbye. Oh, happy Valentine's Day!"

She imagined him tossing his hair back. Or it'd be in a pony tail, if he'd been working out with a client. Sweaty, talkative, peering, looking inside you. "Every guy has an angle," Stephanie once said. "The worst ones pretend they don't. And how do you know?"

I) Out of the Past (Previously Frozen)

"You never lose control, do you?" Wayne once said to her.

"And the choice is?" she'd replied. Sooner or later, all the men tried to take charge, or worse, talked about wanting children, like the fellow food-service manager she'd met at a conference, a somewhat pared-down version of Luciano Pavarotti. *Arrivederci*, she thought. She'd learned a great deal about control when Wayne had almost squandered their money on a gourmet foods store — in a region where cholesterol was a food group. "You didn't do enough marketing research," she'd said.

"That's not the problem. It's your total lack of interest in what I do." Which didn't account, however, for why he'd withdrawn thousands from their joint account, or why he despised the work she did for the school. "You're just a fancy short order cook," he'd said.

Jamey, at least, found her work fascinating. "Think of all the good you do," he'd told her, his dark hair almost mirroring her own, almost touching his shoulders, eyes glittering, his physique a walking advertisement for his work as a personal trainer.

J) Kisses & Hugs (Loose)

Now she had to balance the need to recognize the saint's day while also assuaging the parents who complained about sweets being too available. She thought about Big Ed, who'd loved his candies. She was moved to think of calling her own father still hale and active, retired from IBM, now selling food-based supplements online with his wife, Beth's mother, who had been a nurse ("I can't tell you how many people I've seen dying of malnutrition when they thought they were just fine"). Both of Beth's parents measuring the world's literal substance as a way of proving that intelligence and order were all one needed for a good life. For life itself. Their lack of irony (or even, someone once said, imagination) something that Beth and her sister Evelyn had inherited, along with a fierce competence at whatever interested them. Evelyn enjoying the close scrutiny of things, while Beth loved to organize events and people, telling her parents where to sit during the little play luncheons she arranged in the backyard, where Evelyn was always asking, "What do you call this?" holding up a weed or a beetle. It was only years later they met their Aunt Flo, just out of prison, where she'd served eight years for a bombing in Atlantic City during the Vietnam War. "Believe me," she used to say, her bleached hair bright in the sunlight, "you better not listen to what a man tells you, unless you have proof." Whatever proof was. "Oh, I'll never get married, not me." She worked now as a waitress in one of the casino restaurants in Atlantic City.

There was so much to do today, laying out little cups with foil-wrapped chocolate kisses and candy hearts that said, "I love you." The girls of a sixth-grade class had drawn names from their teacher's manila envelope, pairing themselves off randomly with a boy with whom they would spend the day working together. Each student would have the name of his or her partner written on sticky tape and attached to their sleeve. "This is an ancient practice," their teacher, Ms. Salvati said. "It goes back to Ancient Rome. Wearing your heart on your sleeve." Never mind that Beth learned St. Valentine had been clubbed to death and beheaded.

K) Vegetable Tears (Battered)

Andrea wept terribly when Beth told her of Big Ed's death. "Everyone who loves me dies!" She looked accusingly at her mother, who could see that Andrea was still not convinced that she hadn't driven Andrea's father off for some selfish reason. And now her grandfather was dead, and it was her mother telling her so — but Beth had little time to console her daughter, with lunch time approaching. She hugged Andrea, who froze in her arms.

"I'm so sorry, baby. I know how much you loved him."

"No, you don't."

"Let's talk later, at home, okay?" That would be a tight squeeze, between coming back to school for a parents' committee meeting, then getting to Big Ed's wake.

"I don't want to talk," Andrea said, almost below her mother's range of hearing. "I want to see my baby sister!"

"What?"

"I want to see her before *she* dies! And I want to visit Aunt Evelyn!"

Evelyn — the only relative beside grandparents from her side that Beth could offer Andrea — lived in Boston, where she studied microbes and other things invisible to the eye, including the happiness that eluded her with each marriage. Beth had been determined not to imitate her sister's childless domestic life. Occasionally, she almost remembered their teenage days, their voices hoarse from laughter, and later how much her father had liked Wayne, though her mother kept asking, "Are you sure?" perhaps still asking the question of herself, living with a husband who weighed an apple before he ate it, to be sure of calories, and who slept with an American Airlines mask to black out the morning light.

"But why do you want to see Aunt Evelyn?"

"I know *she* loves me."

"Oh, sweetie." Beth tried to hug her, but Andrea pulled back, sulking, inconsolable.

Entrees

A) Grilled Cheese With Soup or Salad
The lunch crowd was swarming into the great dining room, students sorting according to their class and friends, settling with giggles at their tables and dipping into the candy hearts and chocolate kisses everywhere. Andrea had already found her little group, quickly surging into communion with her kind, the talk running high and silly, while the boys who sat apart huddled in their own plots and dirty jokes. There must have been three hundred students, some of them lining up for burgers, tuna fish sandwiches, tofu salads, sweet potato fries — which Beth had fought for, over white potatoes — plain green salads, small glass bowls of fruit — real glass, which Beth had insisted upon, instead of Styrofoam — two huge vats of pea soup and alphabet soup, and beyond them the spigots for Coke, Sprite, Diet Coke, root beer, a fifth handle for dispensing ice. Nearby was the cooler for milk, yogurt, soy milk, then a huge revolving tray with puddings and Jello and pecan pie. In front of some foods were signs saying they were peanut-free. The hubbub was deafening, in spite of the high ceiling and its acoustic tiles. Fans spun ever so slowly high overhead, while Letitia, Wanda and Lourmel Touissant — his gold ankh swaying on the chain around his neck as he leaned over the grill — kept replenishing particularly the burgers, Lourmel flipping them, Wanda stuffing them into buns, Letitia packaging them in red-tinted plastic wrap, though some of the students grimaced and asked if the burgers

were *bleeding.* "No, honey," Wanda said, "that's just the color of *love,* how it looks inside your heart. Nice and pink."

B) Slow Roasted Beef (Rare or Well Done, With Two Sides)

After lunch, Beth had just returned from a meeting with the supervisor of services, when Jamey called back, begging for a chance to see her.

"I can meet you after the wake. I can even drive you and Andrea there and wait outside."

"But why? It's just a depressing chore, all of it, that I have to get through."

"You'll be going to the funeral, too, I suppose."

"Yes." She went cold. She hadn't really thought about the funeral at all. Probably the last one she'd attended was her grandmother's several years ago. Who would she ride with, going to the cemetery? Wayne and his two brothers would be with their mother. Beth would be the ex, in her Civic, tired, dry-eyed, her daughter crying. Then the grave site. An Army color guard. Later, the carefully folded flag presented to Marjorie, supported on each side by Wayne and Alan. Her expression totally blank.

"I could drive you to the funeral, you know."

"Oh, Jamey..." At that moment she was startled by shouting outside in the loading area. There was a loud *pop*, like a balloon bursting. Then screams and more shouting. Someone was yelling, "Call 911! Call 911!" Beth ran outside. She had to push through a group of workers. On the floor near the delivery driveway was a tall black man lying on his face, a trickle of blood emanating from his right ear. His hands were spread out in a grotesque hallelujah pose. Near his right hand was a small caliber automatic. Tangled in the fingers of his left hand were a gold ankh and its broken chain. Deeper in the storage room stood Douglas, with a bleeding Ky in his arms. Ky's wife was shrieking. Behind them stood Wanda, with Letitia clutching the big woman's arm, tears streaming down her face, her hand over her mouth. She was trembling. "Lay him down, put him down," someone commanded Douglas, whose long hair had swept over the bloody chest of Ky and was blood-tipped as he tried to swing it back with a motion of his head. In the driveway stood one of the kitchen workers, his short, powerful arms at his sides, a two-by-four still in his right hand, his eyes dazed.

Wanda, holding Letitia close, explained. "That man, it was that man, he's a bad man." Beth remembered when Wanda had poked her head into the office earlier. *Miz Romney, you want these leftovers or can we take them home?* Wanda had held up a tray of burgers and sandwiches. One of the perks for the employees was that they could take these things home to their families, though Beth had learned from Wanda that Letitia's boyfriend would have none of it. *I don't want no white folks' leavin's and we ain't gonna eat none of that stuff!* More than once, Letitia had sported a facial bruise, her mood deep and lonely, as Beth harangued her, trying not to, trying to convince the woman that there was a job to do that was independent of her personal turmoil. That the outside, objective needs of the job might even save her — as it had so often Beth herself.

C) Veal Cutlet (With Two Sides)

Wanda pointed to the man lying on the floor. He had come home in the afternoon to find a note from Letitia saying she was leaving him. Her clothes had already been moved to her aunt's apartment in Marietta, though she hadn't revealed that — nor had she told any of her co-workers — and she hoped he would go back to the VA medical center and get the help he needed. Whether it was from the expended uranium in the artillery shells he'd been exposed to in the Gulf War, or the chemicals in his body from trying — as ordered — to immunize himself against a gas attack, Edward Denmark III, the man on the ground, who got sporadic work in the service departments of car dealers or in local gas stations, had once been the kind of person a woman was drawn to — good-natured, humorous, his long legs hanging over the mattress — until his digestion went bad, his sleep was devastated, he grew suspicious, he drank, he swore, he hit Letitia and the next day begged forgiveness. Beth understood more of the story than Letitia would have imagined. "He came in here," Wanda went on, pointing to the entrance into the storage room, where the trucks backed up, "wavin' this pistol and don't you know Tisha is there, not in the kitchen, she's there, listenin' to Ky about some inventory stuff, and in he comes, Edward, wavin' his pistol, and Ky puts himself in front of Tisha and says — you know how funny he talks—'You no belong here! You go away! I call police!' And Edward shoots him!" A kitchen worker had then crept up behind Denmark and struck him down with the two-by-four he still held in his hand. As Denmark fell to the ground, he'd reached out where Letitia's co-worker Lourmel had been standing paralyzed with fear, and pulled the ankh and the chain from Lourmel's neck. Hearing the shot, Douglas had rushed into the storage room and lifted Ky in his arms.

D) Spaghetti and Turkey Meatballs
The bullet had struck Ky's clavicle, shattering it, but the full force of the bullet had been deflected just enough so that Ky's life was not in immediate danger. He had passed out, with Douglas holding him and yelling at the fallen Edward Denmark, "You crazy son of a bitch! You fuckin' nut case!" Ky's wife was sobbing into her hands now, then stroking her husband's face. The kitchen worker let his two-by-four drop and put some empty burlap sacks on the ground and directed Douglas to put Ky there. No one much seemed to care about the other man lying on the concrete surface, how he must have suffered at least a concussion or a fractured skull. It was Leitita who wept for him. "Oh, baby," she said, "why couldn't you get help like I told you to?" She went to his prostrate body, but Wanda pulled her back. "No, don't touch him. Wait for the ambulance." "I can't let him lay there like that," Letitia protested, "like some kinda road kill!" She started crying again. The kitchen worker who'd struck him was now sitting on a carton of unsalted cashews, his face in his hands. Two police cars pulled up, lights flashing, followed by two ambulances.

Dessert

A) Strawberries (With Cream or Plain)

"I wish," Andrea told her mother at dinner, "that you didn't work at my school." Six months free of braces — though she still had to wear a retainer at night — Andrea's teeth shone pristine and perfectly aligned, accentuating the increasingly strong line of her jaw as she matured. Her dark unruly hair was gradually being tamed, and tonight, thinking of her grandfather's wake and her appearance there, she had moussed and brushed and combed it into a long undulant curtain on each side of her head, her no-longer-so-narrow face made luminescent — hazel eyes, like her mother's, fixed on one thing at a time as she learned to focus her confidence.

"*Your* school?" Beth responded. "One of the only reasons I work there is to get you free tuition."

"You do it because you like it," Andrea said.

"Oh, you mean, like nearly getting shot to death?"

"You're just saying that to worry me," Andrea replied.

"You think I'm invulnerable?"

"Pretty much!" Then Andrea grew solemn. "I guess grandpa wasn't."

It went that way until dinner was finished and they ate two chocolate kisses and Beth told her when she would return from the parents' committee meeting and then they would go to Big Ed's wake. She'd had time to mow the small front lawn of this house she'd bought last year with a thirty-year mortgage. Time to try to make herself small as various male neighbors drove by or came walking their dogs, all of them sniffing the scent of a young, divorced woman that wafted over the neighborhood like recently opened honeysuckle.

B) Crème Brulée
It all seemed so anticlimactic. Death, then two near-deaths — Edward Denmark had almost regained consciousness as they carried him out on the stretcher, only to fall unconscious again. "He's goin' away now, for sure," Wanda had said. All Beth could wonder was how close Wayne had come to such an action. She imagined herself shot, lying on her back, the pewter pendant he had purchased for their anniversary steeped in the blood welling up from her fragmented sternum, as he stood looking down, his long, moody face crumpled in defeat.

Just before she left, her sister Evelyn phoned. "Andrea called me," she said, her acquired Boston *a*'s still alien to Beth's ears. "Are you two okay?" "We're fine," Beth responded. Her sister had the knack of suggesting Beth's child-rearing practices were somehow deficient in warmth. She herself a rail-thin woman in her late forties, sometimes coloring her hair with henna, smart as hell, a kind of whip. Men left her regularly. Not because they feared her mind, Beth always told herself. It was Evelyn's abrupt changes of heart, as if the rigorous discipline of her scientific work needed a certain amount of surrounding chaos she called spontaneity. Beth thought of her own turnover with men. Of Jamey trying so hard to... what?

"Well, she was crying," Evelyn continued.

"She needs to cry," Beth said. "It's called grieving."

C) Tutti Frutti

Before she could get out the door, Jamey called. "You probably think I'm crazy, coming on to you this way, like I'm your husband or something."

"No," she said. "I think you're trying — maybe too hard — to be considerate. But I'm not a widow, you know. Just divorced. And thank God for that."

"I know. Did I ever tell you about my ex, when she poured syrup on my side of the bed, before she left me?"

"No!"

They talked for almost fifteen minutes and he managed to get a laugh or two out of her.

"There," he said, "that's much better. Hearing you more like yourself."

"But you don't know yet what 'myself' is."

"Sure I do."

"Oh, Jamey... not now, please. No more talk. I have to go."

"Okay, sure. I'll call you tomorrow night."

"Okay. Bye"

"Bye."

She waited for him to click off, not sure who was clinging to whom.

D) Dried Fruit and Nuts

Big Ed's delicately rouged cheeks, seen against the white satin pillow his head lay upon, gave the impression of a star in a silent movie that had just been colorized. He was at once himself and something so artificial that even had he suddenly sat erect, no one would have paid much attention, except the funeral director pushing Ed back into place. Looking at the hard candies in a nearby bowl, Beth remembered how Big Ed always enjoyed desserts — unpeeling shiny foil from the chocolate Santas at Christmas. *Keeps me sweet! Ha-ha!* (Wayne at the time trying to smile, avoiding Beth's eyes — having the night before pushed her out of the kitchen after his third bourbon and Coke, as she was trying to arrange things for the next day. *Who cares? You think they appreciate what you do?*) Fatigued from the meeting with the parents' committee and lists and discussions of seating arrangements at commencement and what food to serve, Beth wore a high-necked black dress, a single strand of cultured pearls and matching earrings. Her dark curtain of hair showing a bit of gray, her narrow face showing some lines but lean and driven.

She and Andrea held each other close, staring down at Ed's stiffly arranged black hair that had needed no touching up, its color the same all his adult life, into his death. The backs of his hands hinted at bruises from the various IV needles inserted there, though the mortician's make-up had succeeded in blending bruise and gray tissue into a passable likeness of the hands that Big Ed was known for — broad, muscular, all-encompassing, as he gripped hello to a customer, hands that had balanced joy and despair in a juggling act not even his wife Marjorie had comprehended. For Big Ed had not been a happy man. His three sons distant, none of them interested in the skills that had begun with Ed's tour as a sergeant in the motor pool during the Korean War: Wayne, the now General Foods traveler; Alan the pale, androgynous teacher; Louis, former marine, owner of a bar/lounge, semi-strip joint in Miami — all of them showing more weariness than bereavement, as they stood obediently near the casket in their dark suits, hands crossed in front of them, their mother, Marjorie Romney, sitting in the front row of folding chairs like a figurine someone had forgotten to dust, she seemed so unmoving, so ignored, so porcelain, the odor of cigarette smoke coming off her brittle styled hair and nicotine smudged fingers.

E) Ice Cream (Chocolate, Vanilla, Pistachio)
In a voice raspy and thin, Marjorie addressed Beth and Andrea from her chair. "He loved you both so much. He's leaving you something, you know." "What," Beth said, turning, "Mother Romney, what are you talking about?" Marjorie snuffled into her handkerchief and giggled oddly. "Some of the money he made selling our vacation home on Lake Marion," she said. "The money he would have left Wayne, if he hadn't divorced you. But he always liked you better anyway." She looked at her husband in his casket. Then stared at the empty doorway. "I think he liked you better than me."

"First I've heard of that!" Beth said, remembering the too-intimate squeezes from Big Ed at the family dinners. "He was just being nice to me and Andrea. But you're his wife. The mother of his children. He loved you!" It was too sad and she was feeling uncomfortable. *$200 more a month thrown at the mortgage. The last bills from Andrea's orthodontist. Tires for the car.* She tried not to think about it.

"I *was* his wife," Marjorie said, "but you and he were so much alike."

"Mama," Andrea said, "I'm going to the bathroom."

"Okay, sweetie."

"Oohhh, Grandma," Andrea told Marjorie, "I love you so much." She hugged her as she would a bundle of fragile sticks, then walked toward the stairs leading down into the lounge and restrooms.

The air of the viewing room was heavy with floral odors — some of them from the flowers of friends and family, some sprayed by the little man in the dark suit who made sure there were enough chairs, enough mass cards, enough discreet silence, directing the smokers and those just back from the local bar to the rear porch that had open, screened windows. The thick, red, faux Persian carpet emitted a suffocating closeness of barely tamped-down dust. "Mother Romney, you know money was never an issue with us." A small enough lie, as she leaned closer to Marjorie and put a hand on her shoulder, and tried to look into her former mother-in-law's eyes.

"You just have enough for yourself. We don't need anything."

"Oh, but you do," Marjorie said, stung into some kind of attention. "You need Wayne to love you. And he can't. Just like his father couldn't love me."

"You can't just *buy* that!" Beth said.

"Big Ed wanted to leave you something, once Wayne married again," Marjorie pleaded. "It made him feel good about himself, I suppose."

Beth thought of Wayne's young wife, a former dental receptionist, devoting herself to their daughter, who'd already had two operations. Where did that money come from? His company health plan? How much cereal could Wayne sell for General Foods?

"You know" — Marjorie pulled Beth closer — "none of my sons are any good. A waste of time, all I went through giving them birth." She exhaled and Beth detected the sharp/sweet odor of gin, and she remembered the pungent juniper bushes outside Big Ed's house in Peachtree City.

F) Homemade Cookies

Beth looked up to see Andrea talking with her father and his two brothers. Andrea began to cry. She burrowed her head into her father's shoulder. Patting her long, resistant hair, he began crying, too. Beth turned to look at Marjorie, who had sunken into lethargy, as she stared at her husband, who seemed so content, his hands crossed, the untrimmed hairs inside his ears stubbornly revealing themselves. (*Does the hair really grow after death?* Beth had asked her mother at her grandmother's casket. *I suppose.* And Beth had thought, *then how can she be dead?* But when she kissed her on the forehead, her skin was cold as raw steak.) She thought of the wounded Ky in an ICU bed, his wife next to the bed with its rails up, clasping and unclasping her hands in a pulsation of grief. Ky, who had evaded all those bullets and explosions in his boyhood, when headlines referring to the Tet Offensive or later the My Lai massacre had stenciled themselves across the young consciousness of Beth and Wayne, that era epitomized by the photo of a naked child running down a road, her hands over her head, shrieking, whereas Beth's daughter Andrea was now dealing with what? Separation. The rancor between her mother and father that passed as a search for self-fulfillment? She wondered about Letitia's man lying comatose in his own ICU room, next to Ky's, a respirator tube inserted in his mouth, a sheriff's deputy on duty outside the ward, waiting to inform Edward Denmark III, once he regained consciousness, that he was under arrest.

She watched her former husband and her daughter comforting each other, and tried not to guess at the dollar amount she would get from Big Ed's will, remembering how Wayne had started drinking more and more once he failed at the gourmet store project, lost his down payment, and Big Ed had installed himself in Peachtree City with the gloomy Marjorie, who was living too far from her sisters in Ohio. Something about Big Ed's proximity started making Wayne strut into a room half-lit with bourbon and pose as a go-getter, though he used to be a gentler kind of man, until she became a kind of executive at her school, in a job he'd derided. "You're just the cafeteria lady!" *Ten thousand would be nice.* When had Wayne begun to avoid her? When she came down hard with facts and figures on his fantasy? Or was it just that Big Ed should never have moved to Atlanta? *You're so much alike.* That man lying there, his heart pumped full of colored latex, the dead king, a small stain on his suit jacket from his wife's tears — or the moisturizing lotion imperfectly absorbed by her hands.

THE ROAD
TO POMPEII

IN THE LAST phase of the tour in Italy led by Professor Maria Elana, there was no way to know just what would happen on the bus trip from Rome to Pompeii, but Katherine was taking no chances, especially after Lorraine, one of their party, had said to Edgar, "I don't want you spoiling this trip for me tomorrow." She had already complained about the students on the tour drinking too much, until Maria Elana explained, "They're all over twenty-one," which must have been a lie, Lorraine insisted. But the students — three young women and two young men — kept to themselves, taking notes during the day, partying at night. The rest of the group included several people who worked for the college, residents of the rural area it was located in, a professor emeritus, two professors from another college, and a few senior citizens. Katherine went up to Edgar, who was in front of the concierge's station waiting for the others to gather for dinner, and said, "Everyone's worried about you because you're such a piss-ass." She had called him worse in their twenty-five years of marriage.

"What, what?" Edgar threw his arms wide, the Air Force tattoo on his right forearm a blur of blue wings, and he thrust his head forward like a bird. "What are you pickin' on me for?"

Katherine was still angry at him for not taking the bus with her while the others climbed the hill to the Borghese Gardens, and for having insulted the waiter the week before at the restaurant on the Campo in Siena. Edgar had started joking about what "gas" meant in his country, after the waiter had asked, "No gas?" when the group had ordered some *aqua minerale*. The waiter then asked Edgar how old he was and how many languages he spoke, making it immediately clear that he, at twenty-three, spoke five languages and could understand several others. To make matters worse, later, the salmon strips over Edgar's fettuccine were rancid, and when Edgar complained, the waiter said, "That's what you ordered." But the salmon was old, and Katherine made an issue of it by pointing at the dishes everyone else had before them, saying, "good, good, good, and good," then pointing at Edgar's, "bad!" The waiter, it turned out, was a student in international law and not Italian at all. He was Palestinian. "A man without a country," Edgar said, and the group forgave Edgar for what was not after all a cultural blunder but a lesson in arrogance and international strife. Katherine was not convinced.

On other occasions, Edgar drank too much during the late afternoon *pranzo* and giggled loudly. The students shook their heads as he made remarks about the braless women walking briskly past or weaving in and out of traffic on their Motorinos, and Katherine, herself a large woman with a bright young face and gleaming silvery hair, would kick his shin, while Maria Elana twisted her mouth in disapproval. She had already informed Edgar that she would bring him up on charges of sexual harassment if he didn't stop threatening to kiss her. He said it would snap her out of her gloominess over the cold she'd caught on the cramped flight from New York. She — a mere fraction of Katherine's size, being hardly five feet tall, looking up at his flushed face — said that if he touched her once, she'd have him up on charges, though it was unclear just what those charges would be, since they were in Italy and not on the campus of their small college in the suburbs west of the Hudson River. "Oh, you have no sense of humor!" Edgar complained.

He had also talked the ears off the two professors from another college, Martin Ostler, a tall, narrow, frail man, and his robust wife Alexis — the only two seriously religious people on the tour — when they were in the Sistine Chapel, Edgar ignoring the signs that asked for silence and commenting on the manliness of Michelangelo's women. He had been even worse, after the lunch in Siena, when they were in the small Dominican church, studying the mummified head of St. Catherine (lit up for a few hundred lire thumbed into a box) that leered out at the faithful. Martin and Alexis were put off stride as Edgar, a technician for a Ford dealer back home, speculated on just how they had removed the head and kept it in such a state. The rest of her body was somewhere in Rome.

During the entire trip, Edgar had been wondering about such things as how they'd mounted a statue on the top of Trajan's Column, or how they'd removed the *scala sancta*, the front stairs from what had been the hall of Pontius Pilate, or how they'd moved the forty-five-foot high bronze doors from the Roman Forum to the church of San Giovanni di Laterano — when he should have been questioning, according to Luke Byquist, a birdlike man with a sharp nose, professor emeritus of mathematics who went on all the trips sponsored by the college — just why the Catholic Church had appropriated so much of the ancient world, including the huge obelisk that the Romans had stolen from Egypt twenty-five hundred years ago.

For Edgar, everything was a matter of physics: to move something from here to there, with a maximum of cunning. In Florence, in the museum of work taken from the Duomo, he'd studied the pulleys and winches that had been used to hoist the slabs of marble and holy statues up the face of the cathedral. In St. Peter's Basilica in Rome, he'd looked up at Michelangelo's dome and compared it to the dome that Michelangelo had designed for a church retro-fitted to an ancient Roman bath. He wondered if the same workmen and the same tools had been used for both. In the meantime, now, in August, in the year that was really the first of the new millennium, 2001 — last year Rome had been mobbed as people marked what was just the end of the twentieth century and Katherine continued to comment on how lucky it was that their twenty-fifth wedding anniversary fell this year, which is why they were taking Maria Elana's trip — Edgar thought of the contemporary marvels in technology like last week's completely self-contained artificial heart transplanted into a man named Robert Tools, whose name seemed so appropriate.

But Katherine knew other things about Edgar. He'd cried in her arms when their first child died, and he'd begged God for another chance. He'd been struck dumb — for once — when they saw the excavations beneath St. Peter's that almost revealed St. Peter's tomb. He'd stood, days earlier, in the courtyard of the Bargello in Florence and looked up at the overhead sky, the swallows flitting back and forth, twittering, and he'd said, "Just imagine, they've been doing that for seven hundred years. How peaceful it all is." It was the kind of remark one expected from Martin Ostler, who had once studied for the priesthood and who had been wrongly diagnosed last year with indigestion when he was really having a heart attack and now was easily winded, his wraith-like presence a pale contrast to his wife, Alexis, who enjoyed long walks and pumped her arms with extraordinary energy. "Just imagine," Martin said, pointing at the swallows, "all the injustice they've seen."

Still, Edgar's boyish lack of restraint was good-hearted, and even Lorraine Pulice — a widowed, middle-aged Motor Vehicle Bureau clerk, whose Visa card had been stolen by gypsy children in Florence when they held up a newspaper and bumped into her — even Lorraine had relented, as they boarded the bus outside the hotel. "You know, Edgar," she said, "what I'm talking about. We all love you." "It's okay, it's okay!" Edgar motioned her ahead of him. Luke Byquist murmured, "*Va bene, va bene,*" practicing his Italian, always adding to Maria Elana's remarks on a monument or a church, as if she never got it right, his bright small eyes fixing on facts like prey. Later, as they drove along the "Highway of the Sun" through Lazio and Campania, 130 kilometers south of Rome, they passed the Montecassino Abbey on its hill, and the guide narrated a brief history. *St. Benedict founded his order there. The monastery was sacked by the Longobards in 584, burned by the Saracens in 883, mostly ruined by an earthquake in 1349, bombed repeatedly from January to May in 1944, when it was leveled, though it has since been rebuilt.* "You think there's a message being sent about this place?" Edgar asked, ignoring the swirl of religion and politics the guide had been trying to explain. "It has a rich history in the annals of the church," Martin said. "Yes," Luke said, "and it's always been an important strategic location." "For what?" Katherine intervened. "Why is history always about war?" "It's certainly not what the Benedictines would have preferred," Martin said. "*Sic transit gloria mundi,*" Luke added, nodding like one of those toy birds that dip toward water. Edgar, whose sense of history was largely derived from TV specials and films, was thinking about a movie with Robert Mitchum in which American troops tried again and again an assault on the abbey, only to be thrown back. "It made a good movie," he said.

Everything was going well as they approached Posillipo and the Bay of Naples, with a view of Vesuvius in the distance, until the bus pulled into a rest stop where they picked up a number of Japanese tourists whose bus had broken down — just as Edgar was reading about the erotic frescoes on the walls of homes and the brothels in Pompeii, how they'd been dug out from under eighteen feet of ash and little stones. Soon they'd be in the Naples National Archaeological Museum to see what had been transported from the ruined city.

Suddenly, looking at the Japanese men helping their wives board the bus, cameras swinging from their necks, cloth sun hats pulled low on their heads, speaking rapidly while at the same time avoiding eye contact with the Americans on the bus, Edgar remembered his father so grievously wounded at Tarawa during the war in the Pacific — something he hadn't thought about in years. *Look at them, behaving just like anyone else, not knowing how Dad suffered. And probably not caring!* He sank himself deeper into the brochure's text on the tragedy of Pompeii, the eruption of Vesuvius that had begun at noon, August 24, 79 A.D., the citizens buried under falling ash that asphyxiated them. Looking at the Japanese couples on the bus, he thought of Hiroshima. Nagasaki. *Good!*

Imagining that fateful afternoon in Pompeii, where the wells had mysteriously dried up ten days earlier, was all too intense, even though Edgar's curiosity, perhaps even his lust, had been stimulated by the material on the erotic frescoes and statues, the stone phalluses inscribed with *Hic Habitat Felicitas*, "Here Resides Happiness." He thought about his father's death, the two years of a little oxygen tank trailing him wherever he went, the plastic mustache that hissed the precious gas into his lungs — emphysema a strange kind of absence that drew vitality into itself. But life went on, as Katherine always reminded him, and now their oldest daughter, Doreen, would be having her first baby very soon.

Once arrived in the Museo Archeologico Nazionale, where Maria Elana had paid everyone's admission fee, Edgar, Luke and Lorraine sought out the *camera segreta*, the secret room housing the erotic materials from Pompeii that were no longer kept hidden from the ordinary public. For a small charge, one could book a twenty-minute tour, after signing up at a kiosk for a particular time. "I don't need to see any of that," Katherine told Edgar. She'd always been more of a church-going Catholic than he was — having gotten tickets for an audience with the pope that most members of the tour had attended last week, after having the contents of their backpacks examined outside the Basilica ("You think this is a bomb?" Edgar asked the frowning guard, as he held up an apple) — but she'd never been a prude, enfolding him in her generous, large embrace whenever they could get some privacy from their one remaining daughter at home. Edgar had never been a particularly imaginative lover, but he prided himself on his stamina. Katherine would always poke him when he made fun of the Viagra commercials on TV, putting a finger to her lips, lest their daughter doing high school homework in her room — her TV probably tuned to the same channel — would hear him say, "It's only limp dick. It's not a *disease*." On the bus, looking at the same material on Pompeii, Luke, brimming with information, had turned to Edgar and said, "You know, the phallus was seen as a token of good fortune." Edgar, at the time looking at a reproduction of Priapus weighing his enormously swollen penis in the pan of a scale, said, "Then this guy must be the luckiest man on earth." But, finally, in this place kept hidden from the public for so long, what was there to see in the statue of a satyr copulating with a goat? Or the stone erection penetrating a sitting woman with her legs spread wide on a bas relief frieze? "The Faun's Kiss"? "The Surprised Nymph"? "The God Pan on a Mule"? The endless votive phalluses? Edgar knew that he really felt desire only with Katherine, only with something in other women or in reproductions that reminded him of her abundant thighs, her erect rosy nipples, her breasts warm and full in his hands as he held her from behind, the slope of her ass when she turned on her side, her moist soft interior that he knew so well. He hoped they could make love back in their hotel room.

"Time to go," Maria Elana said, warily eyeing Edgar and Luke as they emerged from the secret room. "Wow," Edgar said. "I can't believe they charge for that. I've seen better on HBO." Katherine slapped him on the arm.

Back in the bus, Edgar read the account of the eruption provided by Pliny the Younger, whose uncle had perished trying to save others. *As the buildings of Pompeii swayed, there was confusion whether to stay inside or to risk going outdoors, while something seemed to pound with great force at the base of the walls, blow after blow. The air had grown dense with smoke and ash, the light blotted out. If they left the buildings, they'd be hit by falling stones. If they stayed, they risked being buried alive. It was a matter of what death they feared the most, though some were already tying pillows to their heads as protection against the debris that was beginning to rain down everywhere.*

The bus slowed and the English-speaking guide, a woman with a German accent, said they would be stopping for lunch before the actual visit to the ruins. The Japanese-speaking guide who had accompanied the displaced Japanese tourists then made her announcement. The restaurant — a small roadside joint, as Edgar called it — required tickets purchased in advance, before ordering at the cafeteria style counter, with the Japanese group staying close together (Edgar, at times, almost pushing into them), as Maria Elana's people drifted off into several groups, one of them the students who had essays to write on Florence and Rome. As had been the case for most of the trip, Edgar and Katherine sat at a table with Luke, Martin and his wife Alexis, Lorraine and Maria Elana. They were relieved that the *melanzane*, the penne, the calamari salad, the squid-ink linguine had already been paid for up front with the tickets purchased from the cashier. It eliminated asking for *conti separati*, separate checks, or *conto insieme*, a single check, though Luke had corrected Maria Elana and said, "It's called *conto unico*," with Lorraine always doing the arithmetic for what people owed, her work at the Motor Vehicle Bureau having trained her for accuracy and, it would seem, moral rectitude.

This afternoon, once the food was brought, the mood lightened — Edgar, after tasting his calamari, held up his right hand, making the okay sign, his thumb and bent forefinger shaping a zero, the remaining fingers spread wide. "In Japan," Martin offered, "that means you have no money. It happened to me once when I was dining with some Japanese colleagues in Tokyo and I made that sign to the waiter, thinking to tell him how good the meal was. Everyone panicked and started reaching for their wallets." The gaunt Martin chuckled. He had in fact traveled to most of the world's capitals as a kind of missionary, before meeting Alexis at a function in Orange County Community College, which was hosting a conference on Christian Studies. They married within two months, too old to have children. Luke, listening patiently to Martin's story about the okay sign, chimed in, "When you make that sign in Munich, you mean 'asshole.' " Everyone laughed. "To each his own," Katherine said. It was one of her favorite expressions, perhaps ever since her one surviving sibling, a sister, had moved in with another woman, and now, years later, was considering adopting a child from Guatemala. "It amazes me," she continued, "how much trouble you can get into outside your own country." She gave Edgar a meaningful look, still not happy that he'd toured the secret room. "What?" he said. "Nothing," she replied, stealing a piece of calamari from his plate. Maria Elana, who had bought a bottle of the local white wine with a picture of Vesuvius on it, passed it around, to many ooh's and ahh's, once the wine was poured and sipped. The restaurant was filling up with Germans, Croats, French, Italians from the north, their buses clogging the parking lot, a polyglot murmur of voices swirling around the tables, an almost visible elixir of history on everyone's lips, even the Japanese, who, though quietly sitting together, nonetheless exuded a curiosity that surpassed politeness or timidity. Katherine caught Edgar sneering at them. "What's your problem?" she said. "Don't embarrass me."

Nearby, though it had been buried for hundreds of years, was the site of a tragedy that had occurred forty-six years after the death of Christ, a city now revealed intact, its streets, shops, public baths, brothels, homes, votive statues and sacred spaces, its amphitheater, everything stimulating a thrill of wonder, before anyone had even arrived to stumble down a sunken, cobbled cart path. *Pompeii had almost disappeared from memory after another eruption of Vesuvius in 203 A.D., and by 1700 only a few scholars knew of its existence, not to mention that Vesuvius had also in 79 A.D. buried the nearby city of Herculaneum under sixty feet of hot mud that once hardened into concrete-like consistency made it almost impossible to retrieve artifacts.* Edgar was finding it difficult to breathe under the weight of all this information.

During the last kilometers before Pompeii, he fell asleep, wondering if his daughter Doreen would deliver her child before summer's end, conjuring images of a baby boy, though Doreen had said that her husband Art Donaghue didn't want to know the sex of their child. There hadn't been a newborn in the family since Doreen's younger sister, Mary Jane. To the gentle sway of the bus and the voices of his companions, as well as a discreet, low mumble from the Japanese passengers, Edgar dreamt of his and Katherine's first child, Ted, born with a digestive system so undeveloped that eventually he died of malnutrition despite the best efforts of Good Samaritan Hospital and all their IV feedings. In the dream, little Ted was as small and pale as he'd always been, only a large red birthmark had appeared on his left cheek, and Edgar kept trying to wipe it away, his son's eyes squinched shut, the tubes inserted in his nostrils and taped to his chest periodically leaping as if alive. "Oh, God!" Edgar woke sweating. Katherine, who had also been dozing, started awake. "What?" she said, putting her hand on his tattooed arm, where the wings of his drunken youth remained spread for take-off. "I dreamt of Ted," he said, almost shaking. "It was too real!" He couldn't shake off a premonition of disaster.

Every year on Ted's birthday the family toasted him. Katherine had composed her email address as a series of initials of the names of all her children, including Ted's, but his presence had been so nearly symbolic that neither of his parents had felt very close to him for a long time. Today, on the bus, that had changed. "I think it's all this stuff on Pompeii," Katherine said. "It's like reading about the Holocaust. It gets into your blood. It makes the day dark. It frightens the crap out of me. One day you're making lunch and suddenly the world ends." "C'mere," Edgar said. He raised his wife's hand to his lips and held it there. "We did everything we could," he reminded her. "It was so long ago, sometimes I think it never happened." "Oh, it happened," Katherine insisted, thinking of the pregnancy, the ominous feeling all along that something wasn't right, the young, stupid doctor who kept assuring her everything was fine, and she had done her best to believe him, since he was a provider in her medical plan. Some of that feeling had returned. "It happened," she repeated. "You never think it'll happen to you."

The bus lurched to the right, turned, straightened, and they pulled into a large parking area. The city of Pompeii was instantly there, all of it, as clear and perfectly formed as the development down the road from where Edgar and Katherine lived in Rockland County. Edgar couldn't help thinking of Rome's Forum, *its ruined temples and basilicas, the originals so devastated by Visigoths and Vandals that what was once the Forum, Rome the city of marble built by Augustus, became known as the Cow Pasture.* Now, here, in front of him, was a city plucked from ashes.

As people left the bus, Edgar was aware of his own losses — not just the baby Ted but his brother Dave lost to Vietnam, his sister Maureen to mental illness, drugged and shuffling in a state institution, though now she lived in Newburgh apparently self-sufficient. He was always afraid to contact her. When his little son died, Edgar had felt pursued — but then Doreen was born, a perfect, plump baby, good natured and an early walker. Some years later came Mary Jane, surprising Katherine, who'd been told that her uterus was showing disease. Eventually, she had a hysterectomy, saying, "My uterus is probably floating somewhere in the Hudson," causing Edgar to almost gag. "Ugh!" he said. "Why do you talk that way?" Now, Doreen had found a nice young man in Art Donaghue, who'd graduated from the Culinary Institute of America and was in training as a sous chef at the Windows on the World restaurant, in the World Trade Center in Manhattan, where he was also getting part-time work for Doreen's sister. Art — fated to make a living with his hands in a manner so different from Edgar and his father: men who'd come home tired, sometimes smelling of beer, their bodies aching.

Edgar was holding conspicuously back from the Japanese group. "They won't bite, you know," Katherine said. "I just don't feel comfortable," he replied. "I can't help it." "Let's just move," she said. "I want to see everything." Wrong, something seemed wrong to Edgar. He wanted to pull one of the Japanese men aside and say, "You think you had it bad, because we bombed you? Let me tell you something..."

They entered through the Porta Marina, a gateway that had once been near the sea, which was now more than a kilometer distant. There a passage for pedestrians and one for carts and carriages. Luke Byquist observed, "This is probably where everyone came to escape the eruption, trying to get to the water.

It didn't help." They began walking along the paved road made of basalt blocks, imbedded here and there with numerous small white stones that, Katherine read from her brochure, reflected light (if there was any!) during the dark hours for people to find their way. There were also stepping stones in the middle of the path, for pedestrians to ford the sunken road during heavy rains or the slops that people tossed there. The sun was strong and Edgar pulled on his baseball cap, while Katherine wore her all-purpose blue denim hat that cast shadow over her face and all around her neck. They could hear Martin explaining to Alexis that the space up ahead to their right had once been the site of the temple of Venus, patron goddess of Pompeii. *It had already been damaged in the earthquake of 62 A.D., before it was damaged further seventeen years later. The worst hit of all was during World War II when its excavation was totally destroyed by an Allied bomb that, it was rumored, was originally meant for the crater of Vesuvius, to trigger an eruption.*

"Wouldn't you know it," Katherine said to Edgar, when after a while they reached the great open space of Pompeii's Forum, "that it was the goddess who was destroyed and not that guy." She pointed to the Temple of Apollo, the statue showing the god mid-stride, his left arm extended — a reproduction of the original they'd just seen in the Museo Archeologico Nazionale. At least that she had seen, while Edgar was looking at the art in the secret room. All around them was the grassy space where worshippers had once stood, at a lower level than the priests who looked down from their holy seclusion in the temple itself. Edgar thought of the church of his youth, a priest at mass lifting the host, while everyone pounded *mea culpa* with knuckles on chest and refrained from looking up at the mystery of transubstantiation. He wondered what had happened to those feelings he used to have. The awed internal hush of being that followed a boy home to breakfast and dissolved amid the chatter of family. "Boy, this could be some tennis court," he said. "Or maybe this is where they sacrificed virgins... if they could find any!" He snorted. "Get your mind out of the gutter," Katherine said. Luke joined them and commented on the area across the forum that belonged to the Building of Eumachia, which had a surviving entrance and ornate marble. Eumachia, a priestess, had paid for the building ("With what?" Edgar thought), which, according to Luke's information, served as a kind of headquarters for dyers and launderers. "All women's work," Katherine said. And she thought of the frescoes and drawings and statues of women offering themselves in various postures to the carnal appetites of men. "Some of this stuff needed destroying," she added.

They were running out of time, Maria Elana warned everyone. With Luke's help, they managed to see the House of the Vettii and its beautiful interiors, and Edgar even had a chance to climb the Tower of Mercury, which gave a view of all the roofless buildings of Pompeii, and perhaps for the first time he was able to envision the hot ash of the eruption falling, igniting the roofs that crashed in upon the trembling inhabitants, people screaming useless directions at each other, every attempt at help suffocated. At the end of the forum, they visited the Temple of Jupiter, with a triumphal arch on either side, Vesuvius seeming so near that Edgar thought he could touch it. Gone all the marble veneer, gone the bright colors of frescoes and murals, gone the hubbub of citizens and worshippers, gone the warm waters of the public baths and the heated floors, gone the shopkeepers who sold hot foods to pedestrians, gone... Edgar lost his breath thinking about it. "It's really time to go," Katherine said. "This place is making me sick." Edgar was almost dizzy. "It's all so close," he said. "It's all so *here*."

That evening, he made love to Katherine with a desperation that exhausted her. "What's wrong with you? My god!" "Are you complaining," he asked, lying on his back, his hand still on her thigh. "Not exactly. But I'm getting sore." "I can't explain it," he said. "I just feel kind of... wild."

AT THE AIRPORT the next day, they both remarked on how strange it was that they were flying home at noon, the same time of day when Vesuvius erupted, though the actual anniversary was thirteen days away. Everything about Pompeii continued to haunt them. "I guess they had their own Hiroshima," Edgar said, feeling sorry for them in a way he had not been able to extend to the Japanese tourists. "I mean, how can anyone expect such a thing?" "I know," she agreed. "But let's think of today as just another day." In fact, it had been an unusual time of year to book the trip, since most of Rome emptied out during August, but it was the only time available. Edgar bought a ham and cheese *panino*, fearful that he'd be hungry on the long flight. He and Katherine were seated by themselves, pleasantly tired, hardly able to imagine being back home, when they were approached by a quick little bald man in an official looking gray uniform. He asked for their passports and tickets, which they gave up without much thought. "Must be some routine," Edgar said. "We're okay." Twenty minutes later, the man returned. "*Signore* and *signora*, unless you object, we at Alitalia have decided to upgrade you to first class." They were thrilled. When their fellow tour member Lorraine learned of it, she went to the Alitalia counter to plead her special (mostly invented) circumstances (Edgar thought how many pleas like that she'd bounced out of the Motor Vehicle Bureau office) — allergies, acid reflux, a suspicion of food poisoning, the theft of her Visa card — that made it impossible for her to be crushed into a coach seat for all the hours of the flight home. The ticketing agent, a somewhat amused young woman with perfectly arranged hair and the kind of smile that made Italian women renowned, said, "*Signora*, do not worry! Alitalia is pleased to help you!" There were loads of empty seats in first class.

It seemed beyond imagining. Huge seats that reclined almost into beds. A drinks menu, with champagne prominent. Two movies, snacks, meals, pillows, blankets, smiling attendants, with none of the forced circumstances of coach, Lorraine one row ahead of them, preening and sweet, her voice a sing-song of delight, as if she'd never lost a husband, never turned a sour face to the people who approached her counter on the job. It would still be afternoon New York time when they landed at JFK. Edgar reclined, his head deep in his pillow, a blanket pulled to his chin, the first glass of champagne a pleasant bubbly event he kept remembering even as he drifted off to sleep, his hand on Katherine's arm, the whine of the huge engines now a steady hum, then a sudden roar, as the plane turned and climbed to a higher altitude, then leveled off, the curtain drawn on the first class area, so that he almost felt he was in one of the rooms of the house of the Vettii, and if he opened his eyes, he'd be looking at a brilliant red wall with figures in various poses of domestic joy. And Luke Byquist would be yakking about this or that, facts tumbling out of his beak. Edgar fell asleep.

But the dreams were terrible. He was with Ted — who was suddenly a boy of eight or nine with a birth-marked cheek — Ted's young sisters Doreen and Mary Jane, and their mother, Katherine, an ominous rumble in the background, as Vesuvius blew out its heart. He woke trembling, almost weeping, remembering the plaster figures of people dying on their knees, out of breath on their backs, clutching their throats, when Vesuvius asphyxiated a population that had one hour earlier been going about its business. He imagined plaster casts of Katherine and himself, his hands caught mid-air that had been holding a sheet or a toga over Katherine's head to shield her from the falling ash, when it was really the gray fume and gas that was choking the life out of them both, the sea being sucked away, leaving ships beached and crumbling, the Temple of Apollo, the promise of the God gradually disappearing under a mountain of stuff collapsing from the cloud shaped like a umbrella pine tree that had risen over the city. "What is wrong with you?" Katherine asked. "I'm dreaming again." His forehead was beaded with sweat. He kept thinking that there was some way he could save his daughters, though what threatened them, he couldn't say. "C'mere," she said. With the armrest between them folded away, he reached his arm and its tattooed wings around her ample waist, and she held him like a child.

DARLENE
DESCENDING

KYESHA JONES, THE Baptist woman who took Darlene
back and forth to the hospital not only to administer
dialysis but also to discuss salvation and daytime TV
dramas, said, "Isn't it wonderful" — lifting her large
hands toward the ceiling light — "that your husband
carried the name of our Lord?" Darlene reminded her
that her husband's name, Templeton Krist, "rhymes
with 'grist,' you know, as in 'grist for the mill.' Or '*tryst*.'"
Darlene — a once sturdily built woman, still with a lazy
right eye and drooping eyelid, her mouth often twisted
to the side — could not leave her house except for the
visits to the hospital, and was wearing an electronic
surveillance anklet attached by the Dallas police ever

since she had been indicted for shooting Templeton Krist in the head while he was taking a nap. She needed to be on a dialysis machine three times a week, a service that none of the prisons could provide

Two months after her indictment, Darlene fell into a coma. She found herself in a kind of nether region. Damp wisps of seaweed were clinging to her skin and hanging from the trees like imitation Spanish moss. She was walking down a path toward the dimly lit doorway of the house that she and Templeton had bought in Ridgewood, New Jersey — a small home built in the 1950s, with a backyard enclosed by boxwoods and a parlor nearly filled by the baby grand piano where she would play while Templeton sang. She could hear it now, still a bit out of tune, Templeton singing a song from *Oklahoma.* In the driveway was their venerable Dodge Dart. She heard a woman's voice responding in song to Templeton's. She knew the woman had a freckled face, was big-breasted, wore a low-cut sweater and tight slacks that accentuated wide hips. She knew that Templeton wore jeans, his paunch becoming obvious, glasses halfway down his nose. She could envision the metal fillings gleaming in his back molars as he opened his mouth wider for the orotund notes. She was carrying her briefcase. In it was his birthday gift, tickets to a Broadway show, and her father's .22-caliber target-practice handgun. Oh, Templeton would be so happy, and they could stay overnight at the Carlyle Hotel, they could ride in a horse-drawn carriage through Central Park. She tried to brush the seaweed off her arms. Why was she wearing this fuchsia outfit? Why was Templeton calling her name, his voice suddenly thick as if he had a cold — like that time in Atlantic City, when he applied Noxema to her sunburn and confessed that he loved her, and kept blowing his nose and apologizing for it?

Even in this darkness she could still recall the rumor that Templeton had been paid by her father to marry her — when she was working for a life insurance company in the claims division, keeping to herself at home while writing tightly rhymed sonnets. She did try to get out in the world by joining a local arts group, didn't she? That's how she met Templeton, a biochemist known as The Singing Scientist, who performed in local productions. *You don't have to lie flat like that all the time, sweetie, like you're afraid. Ain't nobody gonna hurt you. I know you can hear me. C'mon, turn on your side. See? We gotta keep those kidneys workin'.* Oh, but he promised they would not stay in Dallas forever, even though she knew they were here because Colleen McGuire his co-star from all those productions in Westchester County and New Jersey had signed on with the Dallas Opera Company. Wasn't he always wearing a T-shirt emblazoned with AMICI DI OPERA? How long, how long had she waited for him to be faithful to his word, to return to the Northeast, this man who could sing the trees out of their stiff poses and bring the animals forth from the woods to listen with rapt attention?

Something dark and odorous was roiling the air. She was in her backyard, burying their cat who'd just been put to sleep by the vet. Templeton was in the house, his head in his hands, crying. "I just can't," he'd confessed. He'd always been like that. When they found anything dead in the yard, a baby robin fallen from its nest, or a mouse on its back, stiff with rigor, Templeton would turn away, his hands over his eyes, leaving Darlene or a neighbor to dispose of the remains. To the women in his theater group, this kind of thing made him an *artiste*, and more than once he was offered the shelter of a woman's bed, all those women who glowed on stage, their lives transformed, though Darlene was convinced that Templeton had been faithful until they moved from New Jersey to Hartsdale, in Westchester County, which is where she was now, standing at the big four-corners intersection, the air heavy with car exhaust, the sign on a nearby telephone pole advertising *The Most Happy Fella*, starring Templeton Krist and Colleen McGuire. She could feel the sun burning through the haze and was having trouble breathing. She knew that as she stood, waiting for the WALK sign to light up so she could cross Central Park Avenue, Templeton was at this moment in their condo (so much easier to maintain than a house in New Jersey), caressing Colleen, a woman who'd left a trail of husbands and lovers behind her like sacks fallen from a truck. Darlene reached the building and rose in the elevator to the fifth floor, still finding it difficult to breathe. She slipped quietly into the apartment, into the bedroom, and with her ring of keys beat and scraped Templeton on his naked back, even as he was pumping away. The woman beneath him screamed. It was the cleaning lady, who struggled out from under Templeton and was standing now, a black woman with beautiful eyes, holding a towel to her body, saying, *I pray for you every day.*

Oh, this was too much! Waiting for the school bus, hair in pigtails, her math homework neatly creased in her school bag, and this irritating boy behind her. She was overweight, clumsy, the object of ridicule, except when it came time for the answers to a quiz. The bus driver always singing, his glasses slipped down his nose as he looked at the children boarding. "Cheer up, kids," he said, "you've got a whole future ahead of you." Then he sang something from Cole Porter that no one could understand. Her father was in the back of the bus, nodding, unshaven, his eyes red-rimmed, something odd on his head, his target-practice pistol in its case, as if he were going to the shooting range, and that's why he wore those puffy black ear guards. Shall I, she thought, shall I give everyone my homework? But it was too late, the plane had taken off, they were on their way to Dallas, she had spilled food down her new blouse, Templeton was reading one of his technical periodicals, his dark hair just beginning to gray, her father's obituary a bookmark in the magazine she'd shoved into the storage pocket on the back of the seat in front of her. What is there to know? she thought. It was cold. Templeton put his hand over hers. "You see, once we're in the air, it's just fine." His clear singer's voice resonating like something she turned up on the stereo (that's what her father had been wearing in the bus — a stereo headset!). "Don't patronize me," she said.

Oh, God, oh, God, she thought. She'd stepped into a puddle and the filthy water had splashed up onto her white slacks. There was nothing she could do, except to pat the stains dry. When she went up in the hospital elevator and got off at Neurology and entered the hospital room, she observed that her mother didn't notice much about her daughter's appearance, being cranked up in bed. She held Darlene's hand and tried to squeeze it. "There," she said, "there." She'd had several discs fused in her spine to alleviate the terrible pains that had affected her legs. "Mother," Darlene asked, "what are you doing here? Why aren't you with your sister in Providence?" "Silly," her mother responded, her white hair let down and encircling her broad face that had so few wrinkles in it, though her eyes had grown watery and her lips trembled. "I came back here to forgive your father. And look what happened to me." "For what? Forgive him for what?" "I came back to forgive him for losing all our money." But she hadn't, Darlene thought. Her mother had never given up the acrimony she'd felt when her husband's electronics business failed and she discovered that almost all her money, as well as his, had gone to creditors. She'd moved to Rhode Island, to a small cottage near Narragansett, where Darlene used to visit her with Templeton. "Yes," her mother continued, "I thought it was time." "But, mother," Darlene said. "you died years ago. After Daddy." "Don't be silly," her mother replied. "You were always such a literal child. Your father will be here any minute." And he was. A hefty man with gentle gray eyes, his shirt threadbare at the elbows — the same shirt he wore when Darlene and Templeton visited in the crumbling apartment on Riverside Drive. After his death, they'd found virtually new clothes hanging in his closet and shirts still in their packaging in his dresser drawers. "Well," he said, "look who's here." He kissed his daughter on the cheek. "Where's Templeton? I thought I just saw him parking the car." "Hi, daddy. Templeton is... Templeton is..." "Hello, everyone!" His voice filled the room. But wherever Darlene turned, she couldn't find him. Now he was singing. The nearly limp flowers in the vase on her mother's bedside table came alive. "Show yourself!" she demanded. "I can't," he said. "I can't."

It must be here, she told herself, digging into the old toy chest. The nursery that still contained her crib and the books she'd learned to read from had a view of an apartment in the building opposite, where a woman was looking back at her. The woman waved. Darlene threw open the window. "Mind your business!" she shouted. The woman began to sing. Templeton was suddenly there too, his arms wide, his head back, his mouth open, the glitter of his silvery amalgam-filled molars almost blinding in the sunlit window, just as they had shone in the lamplight of the den, when he was on the sofa, his jaw hanging slack, the side of his head blown out into a space she imagined as the interior of a giant eye, where she was now, the world blurred all around her, thin red veins like threads in a diaphanous curtain beginning to swell and then empty to a hidden pulse that must be the *thump-thump* of her heart — or the sound of legs hitting the floor and being dragged across a hardwood surface. She could hear Templeton singing, *Why won't you believe me? It's you I adore!* She floated on a darkness like the sea, yet too viscous for that, her eyes open to a nothingness, a voice saying, *Turn over. You can turn over.* And when she did, she sucked in vast amounts of a sugary black tonic like the vitamin-laden syrup of her childhood, when she'd begun to gain weight. The young Templeton reaching inside her bra, though she wouldn't meet him for years yet. *Don't*, she told herself, *don't you give him the satisfaction.* She felt her lungs collapse. Something gill-like in her side opening and closing. The world entirely liquid. And if she opened her mouth, it would fill. Here, his singing couldn't be heard. Here, he couldn't reach her.

What a hill! One never thought of Central Park as being steep. Or of hearing Othello in the nearby open-air theater, *I smote him thus!* The fragrant darkness opening around her like a blossom she emerged from, and she stepped forth sensing his presence in the quiescent trees, the shrubs, something dormant in the air, a newly released pollen that began to fall upon the vacant benches and the chalk-marked path where a child had left her pink *Hello!* They were in the Met again, the greatest museum in the world, he said, the museum mile along the park the only distance you'd ever have to traverse to know human history. *Is there any other kind?* she'd asked, looking around her at the Egyptian tomb artifacts, the promise of an afterlife, the continuation of the senses, bejeweled goblets lifted to a thirst forever unslaked. And here the shattered images of the pharaoh queen destroyed by a jealous nephew. Here the false love of the people. Here the memory of Templeton's first touch at the base of her spine, his hand sliding upwards, his voice like an unknown sustenance she took into her hearing, as if sound shaped itself within her into an image of herself, a tomb figurine, an incarnation of the soul. "Oh, the job is just a job," he'd said. "My real life is in theater." And she wept for the passing of so much beauty, the ocher-tinted slaves pictured in profile on a wall, holding their staffs aloft, the jackal-headed god...

Hissss! A snake sound, she thought. It was just the oxygen tent her mother inhabited. Or was that her father? *Hissss!* "It's pushing the biology of the thing," Templeton had said. "Whether or not you can exceed nature, whether you can improve upon it." It was about the new drug he was developing. Oh, he was so full of himself. So little-boyish daydreaming about fame. So sweet in the way he wrapped the towel about himself after their first love-making, as he went to the kitchen and came back with two flutes of Spanish champagne, holding the tapered stemware up to the light and watching the bubbles rise. "Price is not everything," he said, "that establishes quality." He looked up and down her plump nakedness. "Or pleasure." He was on her in a minute.

Hissss! It was the bicycle's front tire that had been pierced by a thorn. They were on Amelia Island off the Florida coast, for a weeklong holiday. He was huffing and puffing, not used to a bike without gears. She was hardly breaking a sweat. "God, what strong legs you must have," he said. She had that firm kind of overweight, not flabby, no collops of cascading flesh, pneumatic, yes, but taut on the surface, smooth. His tire was now completely flat and they walked together back to the rental center. "It's not you," he said later, lying back. "I think it's my diet. Or those decongestant pills. I'm drying up. No semen. No..." "What about one of your miracle drugs?" she asked. "What about *love*? What about *Colleen McGuire*?" Ten years older than he, that woman with a voice out of Gilbert & Sullivan, its quaver, its fluty highs, its comic alto depths. Its almost phallic drive. *What a shit you are! Really! What a liar. You're so weak!* That noise exploding inside her head. Her ears ringing. A coldness sweeping over her like the fingers of dead slaves.

She could hear him singing a very sad song. He was weeping. In the darkness all around her, the sound of little scurrying feet was like the drumming of a woman's fingernails on a desk. It was her fifth-grade school teacher, Mrs. Johnson, impatient for the answer to a math question she'd put to her, who even then was thinking of him, the boy she'd meet, his hair thick and dark, his smile soothing, his hand outstretched as if to stop whatever trouble was coming toward her, whatever the meanness of Mrs. Johnson's clacking fingernails, because in fact she knew the answer, *It's an imaginary number.* Because they were fated to meet, and she could go back in each of their times to make that happen, to cause him to appear at the desk behind hers, and he'd lean over to whisper, *It's an imaginary number*. And she turned on him, *I know that! I'm not stupid!* His father was already famous for inventing a new kind of plastic wrap that clung to damp surfaces and for... Her own father struggling to keep his business. The huge superstores killing him. *Everything sliding. Why is everything sliding?* She was slipping down a wet wall. She heard him. "Darlene! Darlene! I never meant..." And then the darkness lifted, everything was bright, she stood in a field, Queen Anne's lace and blue cornflowers, purple pokeberry, a giant mullein wavering, her bare ankles speckled red with tiny insect bites, his song suddenly filling the air, the mullein stiffening, the cornflowers heaving to one side, the white lace heads bending over on their slender stalks to make a kind of *O*. "You son of a bitch!" she shouted. "This won't work!"

I know you can hear me, so I'm just gonna keep on talkin'. I told my congregation about you, but they don't know you haven't yet declared yourself and they might think I'm talkin' about the Lord to the wall, because if you don't believe, there ain't no point in anything an' you won't understand it's all about love an' that He loves us no matter what we done.

Hissss!

That evening she saw him on stage for the first time opposite Colleen McGuire in *Hello Dolly*, the woman's voice bursting at the seams. Templeton — playing Horace Vandergelder the wealthy man Dolly had set herself for — had to be aged, a matter of gray hair, penciled crows feet around the eyes, and a little paunch, which he already had. He made love to her when they got home, still in make-up. She knew he was imagining Colleen and she threw herself into it, even faking a Barbra Streisand Jewish accent from the movie, as he came. For a while, she thought it would help to do just that — dress and act like the characters he played opposite. Being the girlish governess Maria from *The Sound of Music* or the young Julie Jordan who falls for Billy Bigelow, the shiftless man who kills himself in *Carousel* and comes back from heaven to perform a redeeming last act. Waking up one morning, she'd felt ashamed. Humiliated. Not that she hadn't enjoyed the sexual fantasies... until he lost interest. And it was clear that he and Colleen were doing more than rehearse. She heard him singing again. Like Billy Bigelow returning from the dead. Here to save the daughter they never had. So it must be to save her, Darlene, his wife, the woman he... "Forget it!" she yelled.

Pain, is this pain, a hollowness invading her legs, so she can hardly walk up the path to their home near Fair Park and the Garden Center and the Music Hall in Dallas? They'd just closed on the mortgage. "We'll get a new kitchen, I promise," he said. "I don't care about the kitchen," she replied. "I want a new life." "But we're here, it's all new!" "I want you to love me. Just me." Her voice was mournful. Is it so terrible to be alone? And where was he? She imagined him wandering in a vacant theater, looking up and down the aisles, then going up the little stairs that led to the stage, turning to look at all the empty seats. "I'm here," she called out. "I'm right here!" She sounded like a five-year-old playing hide and seek.

She was floating again. Remembering how she ran the correspondence section of a big insurance company, teaching young women how to sound concerned, when their real job was to deny claims. It was like marriage. It was like Templeton coming home from his job, saying his supervisor didn't know any science, he was just a money man, they'd wind up with a drug that terminated people — and all she felt was fatigue with people's complaints, boredom in spite of her new Armani outfits, the bi-weekly facials, her weight creeping up ever so slowly. He'd run off to rehearsals and come home late, the poems she was writing getting tighter and tighter, shrinking to epigrams that off-rhymed *hex* and *crux,* though sometimes she wandered into an Elizabethan style and spoke of the moon, something obscene always trying to insinuate itself into the florid harmonies of a bygone age. "You're so talented," he would say, standing behind her, reading the page in her typewriter, reaching down to cup her breasts, just as she hunted for a word to rhyme with *flume... buffoon... some scrotum...* "And you, too, darling," she would say, turning to him, especially after rehearsals, pressing at his erection with her open palm, as if to push it back into its socket. Oh, she loved him! She did! Isn't that why she leaned over him when he was sleeping and... what must he have been dreaming?

A kind of fire was fingering her groin. She was nauseous. Her womb felt bloated. She bent over on herself. Three miscarriages and still she was weighted down with a life within her that whispered into her dreams. The names of girls — *Melanie, Claudia, Penelope* — written on the pad at her bedside table, though she hadn't remembered doing that during the night. He would read them over breakfast, tears in his eyes, Pagliacci with the *Times* in one hand, a lost future in the other, his utter phoniness worse than anything he simulated on stage. She snatched the names away from him. "Don't make me sick," she said, "with your *feelings.*" "I just can't win with you, can I?" he said. It was true. He couldn't. She knew it. She was rolling from side to side. *I'm just gonna make you more comfortable, sweetie. Then I'm gonna read to you from the papers this story how a woman saw Jesus in an elevator. Up and up, we all goin' up. To Him.*

No. She had to go down. That's where he was. That's where she'd put him. He'd come home in tears after Colleen's collapse on the tennis court. Not that he ever played, being soft in his body now, almost womanish. Why had a person of Colleen's size (and age!) been racing about on a court in Texas heat? What a relief! They could return to the Northeast now. She had to find him. It would be okay now. There were plenty of tech companies in New Jersey or Manhattan, laboratories on Long Island, new glass buildings in Westchester County that housed the latest equipment. "Where are you?" she called. It was like shouting down a well, her echo swirling about. "This is my home now," he'd said. "Our home." Praising Dallas neighborhoods like Deep Ellum for their variety. She knew what it was. He couldn't leave the cemetery where Colleen had been laid to rest. He'd rather stare down at that tombstone than take his wife by the hand back to where they'd been nearly happy, her parents still alive, his early years of success as a scientist and a tenor, before they moved to that house in Ridgewood and something went sour. What was it he wanted — adoration? Applause? It sounded so cheap. Something out of a celebrity scandal tabloid. Fame. Oh, she gave him fame, all right.

Why you sweating so much, sweetie? What are you doin' wherever you are that you so tired out? You just dream lovely dreams how you gonna come back to me. Just listen to this nice music, these people singin' how they be saved. The air stirred around her. He was singing. It was something from Wagner, she knew that, something he would never have attempted, something only a heldentenor of great girth could have sent soaring upward to the balcony seats in a vast theater, something out of *Tristan und Isolde,* and she realized he was not looking for her, though she tried to imagine herself dying in his arms. But where was he? Down, he was further down, and she descended, a loose hospital gown fluttering about her. She remembered how in restaurants he would tuck the napkin under his chin and laugh when she splashed a bit of sauce on herself or when the butter was so hard that she began hacking at it. He'd had a subtle way with the physical world. He could transfer the last of the olive oil into a cruet, never spilling a drop. He could thread a needle on the first attempt, not needing his glasses. He could find whatever she would drop, whether it rolled under the couch or slipped down the drain and got stuck in the elbow-shaped pipe under the sink. Twice she'd slipped on the front walk in the winter, until he put down a long narrow carpet that their friends joked about. His friends. Her own had gradually fallen away, people she'd known since grade school, among them a teacher, a middle-school principal, a dentist, a corporate executive, but none of them so entranced with Templeton's singing career that they would attend his performances or cut out articles about musical theater. All *his* friends did that. "But, sweetie," her old roommate from college said, "I thought he was a scientist. He talks about nothing but all these shows. I mean, it's only entertainment.

Whatever do you do with yourself?" Without saying, "*No children?*"

She kept falling, facing the side of a mountain. It was impossible to tell whether she was going up or down, but she could feel everything pushing up into her throat. Slowly, she was descending slowly. He was singing again. Calling at the same time. As if in an operetta, ordinary speech a singsong welter of ephemeral feelings and words that fell from his lips like the husks of *lies*, though she understood the one word that he repeated. The name that wasn't hers. As if by intoning it, he could bring the dark forces up through the earth into the light, create a pathway, a channel, a tunnel, along or through which he and his beloved could unite verb, noun, adjective, stone, tree, bird feather, serpent scale, genitals, mind, heart, stomach in a union of cool flame that did not sear what it healed. She could feel the swelling of time. She could finger the collapse of her breathing. *What do you think you're doin' now? Sweetie, there just ain't no way you can get out that door. But you don't have to. Because He is where you are all the time. I told you that already. I told you He don't have no list you gotta be on for Him to love you. You were born to be saved. Yes, you were. Why He's takin' you in His arms right now.*

"But I'll never leave you," he'd said. "You know why I won't leave *you?*" she returned. "Why I cling to you like skin? Why I'll be with you like the smell of your own excrement? Why I'll pour your coffee every morning and you won't know what's in it? You want to know why?" "Stop, stop, stop, for the love of god, stop it!" he pleaded. "We need to talk!" He sat in the armchair, his face in his hands, like an old man in one of his plays. "You want to know why?" she continued. "Because, believe it or not, I still love you. I'm *doomed* to love you." She wept. And so did he. They made love as if for the first time. But in the morning, she felt nothing. He'd burned it all out of her, she thought. Him and his precious Colleen, they'd set fire to her innocence. But one squeeze of her finger on that sliver of metal, she'd gotten it back. Blood the color of flame!

She was walking now, her hospital gown flowing behind her, its strings coming loose. Soon she'd be naked. Bit by bit, the gown was leaving her. And her memory of when they'd met. Their first home, that small apartment with the leaky faucet in Scarsdale, the Chinese restaurant down the block, how they would sweat in bed after making love and he put ice cubes inside a wash cloth and cooled her back, her thighs. Before that, the honeymoon — the green ocean all around Key West, the bizarre street people, Hemingway's house, and on the way back, the railroad tracks that had broken off from an old hurricane. So sad, the way those tracks wanted to continue but couldn't. A gap, a space, a way of falling into the sea. She was forgetting it all. Before her was a hill. It wasn't very steep, nor did its surface trouble her bare feet. A breeze was building up behind her, and her gown flew off, circling in the air, billowing, swept into the darkness. He was calling her name. Oh, she was ready, she thought. She'd go back. They could... She was forgetting so much! Who was this woman ahead of her? The red hair, the big-woman's walk that was neither a waddle nor a slide but a kind of surging, her hips taut hemispheres beneath a scarlet dress worthy of an ancient Egyptian princess, who would never have been so stout, so outsized, so... Why was she herself unclothed? He was singing, both she and the other woman advancing up the hill. The son of a bitch!

The woman in the red Egyptian garment turned to face her. What had once been handsome in Colleen McGuire's broad face was now swollen and bruised, as if she'd been beaten. Her breasts seemed flat and empty, just so much loose skin beneath her ancient attire. Darlene stared into her eyes, but instead of a sparkling, mischievous blue there were only empty sockets. And when the woman opened her mouth to speak (or sing! Darlene thought, she's going to sing!), there was only a moan and a tongueless cavity. Darlene passed her. Templeton's voice sang out, "Where are you?" But it wasn't him calling and singing. It was Darlene herself. It was her vigor, the power of her love/ hate, that kept him serenading the darkness and its creatures, of which she was one, like the vacant Colleen, both women tethered to each other and to him by a desire not of the body, not of the spirit, but of a vast emptiness, an immobilizing zero-sum logos that was beginning to wrack her consciousness. *You see? I told you there wasn't no kind of foolishness He don't know about. Didn't he suffer everything? Didn't he come to us knowing that he would? You layin' there like you know it all, an' guess what? Sweetie, we don't know nothin'... unless it's just time to go...*

But what if? She was by herself, struggling up a hill, surrounded by dark woods, seeing people in dimly lit copses on either side, some of them gnashing their teeth as they scraped thorns down the sides of their faces, some of them carving letters into their skin with a paring knife, some of them clawing at their mouths, some of them with their shirts torn open, leeches sucking for blood that wasn't there. Here was a man seated, trying to perform fellatio on himself. Here were two women tied back to back, unable to reach one another. Here was a shrieking woman being mounted from behind by a huge Irish wolfhound. A man was eating paper money out of a vat that swirled with grease and cow dung. Two men facing each other were falling on each other's swords again and again. A clown kept ripping off his face, revealing the same clown face beneath. A boy was on fire, blood pouring out of his ears, but he never dropped to the ground. Wrath, envy, lust, greed, what were any of these, she thought, compared to the suffering of the betrayed? All she'd wanted from him was... was...

She could hear him singing behind her. She was making her way up. She knew he was following now. She knew that Colleen had fallen far behind, that woman's blind voice lost in the wind. It would be fine. She would emerge behind the laurels in their backyard. The peonies would be just opening, their soft white flowers displaying themselves. There would be several days of uncollected newspapers in the driveway. Next season's opera offerings would be in the mailbox, the glossy photos of divas, the boxes she could check for *Lucia di Lammermoor, The Magic Flute, Don Giovanni.* She knew he was down there behind her. She could almost hear him puffing, his lack of conditioning what had made him finally a supernumerary, his voice failing, the roles going to younger men, though he always sounded so fine to her, because what she hated she couldn't stop wanting. So she turned, to urge him on. And he was there, his hand reaching for her, the left side of his head a vacancy, his one good eye open and bright. She waved him upward and watched him crumble as he stepped forward, first one leg, then the other turning to ashes, his torso next, though she saw for a last time the old white scar of an appendectomy, then his shoulders fell away, his head fell intact on the ground, one eye open, as he tried to sing.

WAITING FOR Z

IN HIS LITTLE house attached to mine, we cut each other's hair. There's not much of it, both of us balding so that only the hair along the sides keeps growing, though I still have a little on top. We don't talk about my wife and her postcards. *Next stop, Trieste!* She signs herself *Z*. I trim him close, now it's summer and his hat line is perpendicular to his white sideburns. When it's my turn, he tells me my bald spot is pink from sun, I should be careful. Maybe my sister Eve calls from Atlanta, or his granddaughter from San Francisco, or the mechanic calls about the Buick being ready, or Dr. Diek's office for a checkup on his eye they slipped the cataract out of last January. I have an incipient one myself. Distances are getting fuzzy. And I tell him the pilot light is out again on his stove. I smell gas. He says, "Oh," and goes into the kitchen, the scissors still looped on his fingers, and puts his hand on the stovetop over the pilot to see if it's warm. "You're right," he says. I get up, carefully folding the bath towel that is draped around my shoulders so I don't scatter any of the clippings, and go into the kitchen and lift up the stove lid and light the pilot. I know what he's going to say. "I can't smell anything anymore. That's why I feel it with my hand, to see if it's warm. If it's warm, I know the pilot's okay."

She sends postcards. And something in me — calm, accepting, nearly joyous — turns to exultation as I read that Rijeka, once named Fiume and ruled by the poet D'Annunzio after World War I, is just another city, busy with Fiats and pedestrians, graffiti on the plaza wall opposite her hotel. How funny the sign was in Munich, over the escalators of the U-Bahn, *Rechts stehen. Links gehen*. High tea in Kew Gardens, all that butter on the cucumber sandwiches. And the rain. The dolor and dampness of England — not the bucolic village life of a British mystery set in the 1920s, Miss Marple poking about with her wry, acid observations. But Ziva had been restless for a long time. Our son off in Vancouver, working for a film company, his life away from us summoning her blood, a small trumpet calling her forth. All those years caring for an invalid mother. Then she married me. Then she had Mark. After Mark started school, she taught dance as an adjunct at a community college, happy enough, I thought, even when I sold my discount glass and stemware store and retired. A year ago, my mother entered the final stage of her illness, her slow degenerative spiral something that Ziva understood as second nature since her own mother had died of ALS. But she never complained, getting a little blackboard that my mother could write on, and when she could no longer hold the chalk, a magnetic board on which my mother could slide around the block letters that spelled out *water, bathroom, cold,* even *how you*? When my mother died during a horrendous thunderstorm that flooded the driveway, Ziva nodded, saying, "She's not leaving easily." She stood there gazing out the picture window of my parents' little house that is attached to ours by a breezeway, watching the leaves being torn off the branches of the catalpa tree, her lean face showing lines and shadows, her dark eyes dilated, her mouth — the mouth I loved so much — drawn into a speculative pout, as if she were examining a metaphysical issue, when other women would be thinking what to wear at the funeral. Three months later she said, "Harvey, I'm going to leave you for a while. I'm going to travel. By myself." I understood all this. I encouraged her. But now I keep waiting for the last postcard from Paris or Rome, telling me she isn't coming back.

I live only an hour from Lincoln Center and opera, which I attend every year — without Ziva. "It gives me a headache," she said, trying to read the text of the libretto that moves along the little display on the back of the seat in front of her. "It's just so unspontaneous, all this preparation. Like taking a course I'm afraid I will fail." So I go with members of the Opera Club. Today I enjoy the peonies lolling their heavy heads, the pruned apple tree showing little vase-shaped beings that will be apples in September, the hardy hibiscus almost knee high, unfurling, that will be gaping and wrinkled parchment flowers, pink and white, in August, reminding me of the Virgin Islands and bruised mangoes, thudding coconuts and the dank bunker-like cabin we stayed in, where wild donkeys tore open garbage bags and we gasped in the thickening air. Here, outside on the slope that was covered with gravel when we bought the house after my parents could no longer care for theirs in Dutchess County, the silver-filigree maple that Ziva planted has produced a new, slender limb. I remember her cool hand and the wet washcloth she put to my back when I came in from mowing. There's the stokesia, the tall purple liatris, the wild daisies, and rows of alyssum and begonias and impatiens she planted before she left. Not so long ago, I'd found her weeping in front of the TV. "Granny dumping," she said. "They're talking about people who leave their old parents and grandmothers in the street. With notes attached to them."

He comes to the kitchen door, the straw hat with its scalloped edges at once insouciant and something mass-produced to emulate a one-of-a-kind from an artisan south of Texas or California. He knocks as he enters, a tuft of freshly cut chives in his hands, and in his shirt pocket, three red radishes. I know what he will say. "Produce man!" Not the optician who had spent his working life in the Bronx, under the Jerome Avenue El, fitting an increasingly elderly clientele with glasses. I don't remind him it's his daughter-in-law, not his son, who likes radishes. It would be like saying she won't come back to us. And I would have to wonder who's been most important to him. Z. Or myself. Maybe she's traveling with another man. Maybe all our *oohing* and *ahhing* over his vegetable garden is a lot of fakery. Maybe no one should live as long as he is, soon nearly nine decades. Maybe I'm steeped in his bromidrosis and denture odor and my right pinky swollen in the middle joint from arthritis is an admission I can't handle this aloneness. I tell him I'll add the chives to our tuna salad.

WHEN Z WRITES from Avignon, I notice the hair growing down my neck and bristling out from my temples. It's six weeks since our last haircut, and he is worried about tomato worms on his Big Boys. A woodchuck has discovered his butternut squash, so he has sprinkled broken glass around the perimeter of the wire fence — something I wish I could do where Z is, create a no-touching zone around her defined by a ring of glass shards. A theater festival is in progress, artists, writers, students flooding the small city, feasting on the mythology of France, while I think of the women I've known and run a comb through my hair, brooding over its thinness.

When I first met Ziva, she was examining a cut-glass carafe in my store on Central Park Avenue in Yonkers — turning it in her hands, holding it up to the light, looking for flaws. She worked the stopper in and out, twisted it, testing the smoothness of the fit, her long fingers handling it like a musical instrument. She looked up and smiled apologetically. "I once bought a cheap carafe and the stopper never fit right. How do you manage with these prices?" She didn't say it was her mother's carafe, bought decades ago on Canal Street, that it had been knocked to the floor in the last week of her mother's illness, that she was reassembling herself, the shadows under her eyes just beginning to fade, her smile a tentative crease on each side of her mouth, her shag haircut growing long now, the way mourners let their hair grow back after they've shorn themselves in grief. "Because I know where to buy, to begin with," I answered. "No junk!" Right away I wanted to tell her, "Look, you think I'm just a shopkeeper? My father is a published poet (a chapbook anyway), I studied art history, my mother wrote a book on genealogy, I go to the opera, I... I think you're beautiful." And she was. She moved like a dancer, bending at the waist, posing her arms if she needed to retrieve something, or spinning when she turned around, as if someone would catch her, or standing on tip-toe with one leg behind her at a forty-five degree angle, her long, smooth calf a perfect living artifact that one wanted to stroke and stroke — reminding me why I loved glass so much, porcelain, faience — though Ziva was no made thing but a spirit descending into my little store, her blouse clinging and her skirt creasing when she moved to reveal the perfect anatomy of a loved one. Something, perhaps, I had been prone to believe about other women, but this time, this time...

"You want some zucchini?" my father asks me. His basket is full. "If you let them grow too big they're full of seeds." "But there are so many," I complain. "You can make zucchini bread!" he replies. I see the hope in his watery eyes. I see the dimming glitter of his age. I see the uncomplicated physiognomy of the man my mother always said was a good man. "You don't know what other fathers are like," she used to say to me and my sister. *The drinking. The gambling. Never mind what else.* "Dad, I'm no baker. Why don't we just cook them all up into some kind of ragout?" Ziva would have cooed with delight. She would have made bread, salads, pasta, roasts, anything that zucchini could garnish or be imbedded in, the way she used to take me into herself when business was bad. "It's not your fault," she would assure me. She didn't say that before she left, knowing it's what people say when they break up. I could have blamed her very old uncle for leaving her so much money that I found myself saying, "You should do something special for yourself with this." What do you tell a lovely woman in her fifties about searching for herself in foreign places? That some experiences belong to a place and cannot be transported? That the taste of tomatoes in Istanbul will not be the same in New York? That the illusion of change ends with fucking a stranger in Budapest? Her last card spoke about the Tower of London. *I can just imagine Sir Walter Raleigh losing his head here.* That night I woke sweating.

HE HAS TROUBLE getting out of bed this morning. "Damn back," he says. I know how twisted from osteoporosis his spine is, having seen the X-rays of what resembled a serpent beginning to twist and coil. "Maybe you can get the peaches before the raccoons do." Last year he'd waited too long, and when he went out with his basket to harvest the old-style cling peaches, they'd all been eaten, the pits littered everywhere. I hate gardening, but to him, who grew up in the molded and mortared environment of the city, whose family had emigrated from a city without a river or trees, growing vegetables and fruit was like rediscovering Eden. After he moved here, he'd driven my mother crazy with his January seedlings in Styrofoam coffee cups placed on the window sills. Then he bought a Gro light and spread his cups out on the dining room table, the lamp beaming down. She said, "My God, Milton, are we so poor? Is this, what, Tobacco Road? I'm living on a farm here!" "You never know what you're buying," he'd say. "With these, you know everything is clean. No chemicals." It was the kind of thing he'd say about the poets of the Renaissance or the Romantics. "With them, you know what you're getting." (Except he did spray for worms or poke arsenic-coated peanuts into the mole tunnels. And he did like Walt Whitman — "What a guy!" — his eyes bright with an inspiration that at once thrilled and baffled him, until he finally printed up a hundred copies of his own chapbook, maybe thirty poems, which never seemed half-bad. He found a small publisher on Varick Street and got them to print my mother's little book on the history of her family, beginning in a Russian *shtetl*. He actually got copies of it placed in a number of Manhattan literary bookstores, in the history section. In their day, my parents were proud authors.) I remember how at our apartment window in the building near Mosholu Parkway he would look with longing at the green median, the trees, and sigh, "Man was not made to live among rocks and breathe shitty air." We could hear the Woodlawn train pulling into its elevated station — a sound I always associated with childhood, the distant clank and hush of air brakes an urban melody that each night I went to sleep by. "Some day," he said, "we'll go where it's nothing but green." "So," my mother would retaliate, "does this mean I'll have to drive a car? When I can just walk everywhere I need to go right here?" They'd argue about such things. Once, she called him a godless man. "Why," he retaliated, "should I believe in someone who doesn't believe in me?" I go out to the peach trees that are bleeding sugar from their black, gnarled branches and slide the ladder into place. Some of the peaches have dark congealed spots, from a worm of some kind. But most are clean and I easily fill the basket. Then another. The peaches are not entirely ripe, but they'll sit in our windows, taking sun, and in a week's time we'll have peach juice running down our chins.

THE LEAVES ON the silver maple are beginning to turn and Z is in Seattle, visiting a cousin. Soon, she'll go north to see Mark. She's been to Hong Kong. Eaten things she was afraid to know the origin of. Her back hurts from all the hours spent in the coach seats of airplanes. She says she'll be going down to San Francisco to see our niece, my sister's daughter, and from there go to L.A., then cross the desert, later see the pueblos in Arizona, do the Grand Canyon. This is the first time she's written an actual letter and I think the next one or the one after that will be the kiss-off. My father is canning the last of his tomatoes in Mason jars and storing carrots in sand in the garage. I have a butternut squash — one of three that survived the woodchuck — in a basket on top of my refrigerator. Not just any basket, but the Gullah sweet-grass basket that Ziva and I bought in Charleston on our tenth wedding anniversary, when she told me it was definitive, she couldn't have any more children. "Does that upset you?" "We could adopt," I said. "Don't be silly," she replied. "Don't tell me we could adopt a nice Korean baby or go to Africa or Guatemala. This is what is meant to be. We have Mark." Her face, tan from the South Carolina sun, was smooth, her cheekbones more prominent since her weight loss and the hours at the gym, her hair pulled back, her expression resigned, accepting, peaceful — the way she must have been after her mother died. Something had gone out of her. She snuggled into my arms and I suggested we do the harbor tour, go out to Fort Sumter, where the Civil War started. "Sure," she said, pulling away, leaving suddenly a cold space between us, and I felt the shift, the change, a kind of weeping so private it wasn't grief or loneliness or despair. It was like the empty sunlit space on a table where a Steuben vase had once created an etched but voluble silence.

THE FIRST FROST and the parsnips are now sweet, he says, holding up a handful. He's wearing a flannel shirt, a sure sign of the approaching cold, and as he displays the parsnips, I see how sun-speckled his hands are, I want to remind him to wear gloves, that basal cell skin cancer is too frequently a visitor, that he's bent over more than usual, that some days I wish I had not sold the store, that all my friends are getting old and we talk too much about illness, that my son Mark writes to tell me how great his mother looks, but he's not saying what he really thinks. I watch my father waver as he descends the brick stairs leading down from my kitchen door onto the path that goes around Z's garden, her fall crocuses and nodding chrysanthemums. "Dad, are you feeling okay?" "Nap time!" he says. "Listen, let me go next door with you." "Do I look like a cripple?" "No, I just..." "You know what?" he interrupts. "Maybe you should get on a plane and go meet Ziva where she is. You're getting a little strange in the head. A husband should be with his wife." "Dad, this is her special time, for herself. She's done so much for everyone all her life." "Yeah, yeah," he says, stopping on the path, the basket dangling from the crook of his elbow, the plump yellow parsnips and their leafy green tops that can leave acid burns during growing time, "and who doesn't? You think I wanted to come home every night?" He shakes his head. "Get on a plane. Before your wife runs off with someone else." "I'm not going to do that! It's too close. If I do that now, she'll think I don't trust her." "So? Do you?" I see how loose the skin is under his chin, how layer upon layer seems to be cascading down, like something that had been full and was now empty, collapsing on itself. "You know, your mother left me once." He looks out over the garden at the black birch losing its leaves and wipes his mouth on his sleeve. "She left me for Harry, my son of a bitch brother."

I remembered Uncle Harry as the man who gave me two quarters out of the cash register in his dry-goods store whenever I came to visit with my mother, who would be buying something like dish towels or sheets or a tablecloth. He didn't resemble my father much, being thin and long, while my father was square (the way I am), but he went bald the same way, front to back, and his voice had a similar mellow quality. He'd studied the violin, my father literature, both boys entering the business world as something that was expected of them — my father buying into Mosholu Optical after he'd worked there for five years, and his brother Harry buying out old man Levy, whose store had been a staple on Jerome Avenue, under the El, near Gun Hill Road, for as long as anyone could remember. Was it any surprise I went into business myself? "My brother Harry was a ladies man, but your mother didn't know that. She thought he had eyes only for her. Those women who worked for him, he was always in the back, fooling around. He's lucky no husband came around to shoot him. Like I almost did." My father is sitting in his living room, his produce basket on the kitchen table, the parsnips soaking in water. He's already clipped the greens off. His eyes are bright and he talks with a raised fist, suddenly the long fatigue of his years evaporating from him. "Your mother and I weren't married yet. I was working all the time, harder now I was part owner, and all these new styles were coming out, these designer frames, more people asking for contact lenses, and the civil service union was using another vendor for their benefits. It was tight. I used to sit up late reading poetry because I couldn't sleep." As he waves his hands, I can imagine my father talking to a group of students, intoning a poem, an artistic something that had come to me as a love of opera, an admiration for the crystal and porcelains of Steuben, Royal Daulton, Wedgwood, a love of the aesthetic that neither my father nor I, nor my Uncle Harry, who collected old violins, ever brought to more than a secret patina of consciousness, a gleam and furtive craving that some women, like my mother or Ziva, could appreciate as the nonmaterial something that was all the religion we'd ever know. No one in my family went to temple, though we observed Passover, and in his day my father had been an ardent Zionist. "The Bible," he'd say, "the Old Testament, it's about how we survive. God doesn't have a lot to do with it. He's just the history of what we had to do." "You talk like a Communist," my mother said. "Bite your tongue," he replied. But what could possibly have attracted my mother to Uncle Harry enough to leave my father?

"It was all because of one thing," my father says. "One thing." He holds up an index finger. "And it's why you got to get on an airplane and get Ziva where she is." "I don't think so, Dad," I say. "We have a special understanding. You know, Ziva had a life before she met me." "A life? What? She was a sick-room nurse." He grimaces and I protest. "No, no, no. Did you know she wanted to be a choreographer? She was even in a Broadway show once." "I know, I know." My father nods, tired now, being held from a nap by his own insistent narrative. For my benefit. "One thing," he continues, "almost ruined your mother and me. It was a goddamned vase." I think about the Gullah basket in our kitchen. The crystal ice bucket with the etched circles around its base that I'd given Ziva last year, how she looked quizzically at me and said, "Are we switching away from wine to something that needs ice cubes?" "No, no," I protested. "It's to look at." But she was disappointed.

"A fucking vase," my father says. "It was a birthday gift from Harry to your mother. 'For the flowers Milton never brings you,' he said, courting her right there in front of me. Later, your mother said to me, 'You see what it means to be really thoughtful?' 'You know what he wants?' I said. 'What he really wants? All he wants is to get into your pants. Before I do.' She slapped me." I laugh, remembering how petite my mother was, how she must have stood on tiptoe to slap him. And I remember Ziva crying in the middle of the night, after I'd bought the wrong perfume for her birthday. "You don't even know what I wear," she said. Which was true. But an honest mistake. I just can't remember things the way I used to. I couldn't tell her that, a woman who'd seen two mothers into the grave. Now a husband? That's what I told myself. Why didn't I remember her scent? "Your mother stopped seeing me for over two months," my father proceeds. "I was screwed. The love of my life, gone. She wouldn't take my calls. Two letters were returned unopened." And how, I ask myself, could I be writing Ziva if I didn't know where she was from day to day? There were American Express offices where I could leave a letter, but she didn't want that. "That would tie me down," she said.

"So one night, I sat in my car next to a fire hydrant outside her apartment building," my father says. He seems invigorated again, his eighty-seven years a fluid element that had resumed its onward current. "I knew she was dating Harry. That grease ball." The fact that Uncle Harry had died two years ago and that my father had wept profusely at his graveside did nothing now to soothe his jealousy. "Here she comes, walking with Harry, her arm in his, back from somewhere — as if I didn't know they'd been to the movies, his hands all over her." My father shakes his head. "Who could believe it, my own brother." "But you always seemed so good to each other, Uncle Harry and you," I say, trying not to imagine Ziva walking around Puget Sound, looking at the ghostly profile of Mt. Rainer in the distance, a man ten years my junior with his arm around her waist, maybe someone who had followed her from Hong Kong. "Yeah, well, you get old. You learn to forget. We always fought as children. He always wanted to do what I was doing, the squirt." "It's that way with all younger siblings," I say, remembering how my sister Eve used to follow me around, and it was my father who put a stop to it, telling her, "You're a girl. You can't do what your brother does." "Why not?" my mother said, hands on hips, facing him, her jaw jutting forward. "Is he a god?"

"I got out of the car," my father says, "I pointed at Harry there in the street. 'You!' I yelled. 'You're dead to me! You rat!' Your mother started shouting at me, 'Stop this! Stop this now!' 'Admit it,' I said to her, 'you're sleeping with him!' She came right up to me and slapped my face — the second time! 'You're disgusting,' she said, and turned away. I went right after Harry. I grabbed him around the head, the scrawny bastard, I had him in a head lock, like you used to see from Sunnyside Gardens on TV, those wrestlers, I just wanted to break his skull like an egg. You know what he did? He started to cry. Including your mother, she's crying now." He stops and begins to sniffle himself. "What a woman! Sixty years together, she knew me like a book. Even then." I begin thinking, what would I do to keep Ziva? Track her down, threaten her boyfriend with... what? A knife? I couldn't get it on the plane. I look at my hands, a shopkeeper's hands, soft, an artist's hands, though my only art is how I look at things, how I touch things, spun glass, crystal flutes, the long smoothness of Ziva's back, her...

"You see?" my father says. "This is what you have to do, to keep your woman." "What," I say, "put her in a head lock?" He points his finger at me. "Don't make fun." "I know, I know. So what happened?" "There in the street, I went on my knees, I held out my arms and begged her forgiveness." I try not to smile, try not to imagine my father breaking out into song on the Grand Concourse, my mother responding, their voices raised in a duet that shakes the traffic lights loose, stopping traffic, while cops join passersby in a chorus. "Harry went up to her and told her it was okay. He knew she really loved me. He knew she was just going out with him to make me crazy. He knew that, the son of a bitch." I imagine three of them, singing back and forth, dusk settling on the Bronx, the exhaust fumes of buses stinging the nostrils like a salt air, though no ocean is near, only the eternal to and fro of desire... And when, I ask myself, did I ever cry for Ziva? I think of *Evita*. Something cheap and common is trying to enter my brain. "Nine months later, we got married. And just in time. You were born almost exactly nine months from then." He's really tired now, the garden dirt under his fingernails not yet scrubbed out with the brush he keeps on the bathroom sink. He points at me. "Sometimes you have to work at it. I don't mean love, anyone can be in love." Yes, but it's all I care about now. Being in love with Ziva. Wanting her, but trying not to possess her singleness. When that's all I want to do.

SHE SENDS ME a birthday card from L.A. that has on it a picture of Grauman's Chinese Theater and the stars' hand and footprints in the sidewalk. *For My Very Own Star, Who Has Left His Mark on My Heart.* She signs it Z. I think of Zorro. I see her wearing a black mask, dressed in tight pants, wearing a short jacket with studs, Z-ing the air with a sword, I've pulled my shirt open, ready for it. *Zing, zap, zowie.* I feel like such a schmuck that I go into the bathroom and splash cold water on my face. Enough is enough, I think. My father's right. It's time to just go out there and get her. But she can't be in L.A. any longer. What would I do, wander around all the airports from California to Texas? Tell strangers that the crack maple near the shed is bare as bones, I'm looking for my wife, have they seen a tall woman with a loping stride wheeling behind her a small black suitcase with an infinite number of pockets, in one of which is the letter of goodbye that she will mail from a post office near a souvenir stand?

Last night he said, "Harvey, I'm giving up the car. Before I kill somebody." He was sitting opposite me in my living room, in what had become his chair, a recliner that Z and I had purchased at Freight Liquidators, its arms turning dark from the friction of his gardener's forearms. "You having trouble?" I asked. "Almost," he said. "I almost hit a woman carrying a baby in the Shop Rite lot." He was still doing his own shopping, picking up his own prescriptions, even taking the car in for servicing. "You sure?" I said. "Am I sure I'm old? That if I reach across a cup of tea to you my hand shakes like an earthquake? That my legs feel like fallen trees?" He was giving me the Buick, hardly 8,000 miles on it. "You'll never have such a nice car," he said. "Enjoy it." "You sure?" "Are you deaf? I'm sure." He leaned back in his chair, his large hands — that had once adjusted eyeglasses for customers leaning toward him as they would to a doctor, listening to his gentle voice, "How is it now?" — those hands hanging loose and open over the edge of the arm rests, tired of grasping, of holding, of trying to implement his will, while that faculty or organ or whatever it was grew quirky and strange to him, that it should continue its onward momentum, when so much of him wanted to halt. "I just don't care about anything anymore," he said. I could see the widower in him lying back on a phantom couch, folding his hands over his chest, saying, "I need to rest now. Your mother will need me later."

Now I'm afraid to leave him alone. I cancel a meeting of the Opera Club. I take him with me shopping, doing his and mine together, and we have hamburgers at McDonald's, and fries, the same that he and my mother would bring home after one of their junkets — little bags and boxes of this and that left on their kitchen table, while they wolfed down the burgers and fries in their living room. For the first time I feel like a caregiver. Like a wife. I speak in low tones, I try to be soothing. "What the hell's wrong with you?" my father says. "Nothing," I say. "Why is 'nothing' always something? Did you get a card from Ziva? I haven't seen anything in days. Did she run off with somebody? I told you that would happen." He snorts. "Wake up, Harvey!" "Just stop with that stuff," I yell at him. "You think I'm a ten-year-old, you have to be on me all the time? Shit!" "Oof," he says. "Okay. See?" He draws a zippering finger across his closed mouth. I see his hair is bushing out over his ears. I run a hand along the side of my neck, up around my ears. We need a haircut, but I'll be damned if right now I want a pair of scissors in my hand or even the battery-operated clippers. "Okay," I say.

I haven't told him about the last few cards from the desert and places like Taos — with a picture of D. H. Lawrence peering out at me, and all I can think is how his wife Frieda slept with anyone who wore pants, while he groomed himself a Messiah, something I was once drawn to, dreaming of spiritual sex and women who gave themselves totally. These last cards from Z had me in a quandary. She said she was coming home. She missed me. She missed my father's garden. In an actual letter, she confessed that she had trouble sleeping, imagining being next to me. How her body ached for mine. All I could think was, this is the Taos effect. This is Ziva pretending she's in a novel. This is my wife trying not to hurt me, because when she gets home, she'll tell me the truth. That it's all over between us.

I began to think of all the women who had left me. But that was so long ago! What's the matter with me?

He's sitting in the usual chair, in front of his picture window, a bath towel wrapped around his shoulders. "Just a trim, please." He laughs. Then he coughs, a sound too deep in the lungs, his voice thick with catarrh. The early autumn light is still bright enough to fill the room, and the last of the rust-colored chrysanthemums are in a vase on top of his TV. In his hand is the card from Ziva that says she'll be home this Friday, which is in fact today. She's taking a limo from the airport, spending the last of her money. It's so matter of fact it could be acknowledgment of a catalogue order for balloon wine glasses. Or steak knives. I can't help imagining her arrival in a Lincoln Town Car. She's wearing sunglasses, a poncho, jeans, her long legs unfolding in a slow ballet of awakening as she steps onto the driveway, her face shining, more evident streaks of gray in her sun-drenched hair, now more brown than black, a vividly colored travel bag — like something out of New Mexico, rich in ocher and yellow tones — hanging from her shoulder, handcrafted rings glinting on the fingers of her fine-boned hands. She smiles and waves, a woman stepping out of a glossy magazine ad. The image is so strong and I'm so distracted that I pinch my father's ear with the scissors. "Hey!" "Oh, I'm sorry, Dad!" "Pay attention to what you're doing," he says, rubbing his ear. "Is it bleeding?" "No, I just nipped it. It's a little red." "I'm glad you're not my surgeon." "Me, too," I say. This week he'd been in for a physical. The doctor wanted to do a sonogram of his kidneys. "Not a chance," my father said. Then looking at us, "I'll bury both you guys." The doctor, a small man with Einstein hair, shrugged. "It's your body," he said. "You bet," my father replied. I knew he'd been having trouble sleeping and some days his appetite was off. "I'm not an animal, I don't have to gorge myself," he told me. "Besides, I could lose some weight." And he has. He spends more time in his chair, looking out of his picture window, up the driveway, at the huge Douglas firs of the property opposite ours. His eyes, though still glittering, seem opaque, as if he is receding deeper and deeper into himself. I found him asleep one morning in the chair during the time he was usually in his garden, pulling up dead tomato plants or raking in manure for next spring. "Just a nap," he said. "I'm entitled."

"Okay," he says, carefully folding up the towel. "Now you." He stands and takes the white-hair besprinkled towel outside and shakes it over the lawn. I sit in his chair, feeling how warm it is and wondering how I will live when he's gone from me. "Sit up straight," he says, and gives me a little tap on the back of my head. "So, what have you got that's special for Ziva when she comes home?" "Champagne," I say. "Two bottles of Piper Heidsick." "You're not as dumb as you look." And he gives me another tap on the head, the scissors upright on his fingers. My sister called last night and asked him how he was, and he said, "Probably better than you on that crazy job of yours." She runs a Weight Watchers program, still fighting off the pounds herself. She really doesn't like dealing with the public. "I told her," my father used to say, "she's a good-looking woman, like my mother, so a little heavy, so what." Last night, on the phone, he promised he would visit Atlanta, now summer was past. I know he hates flying. "Yeah, yeah," he said. "You pick me up at the airport, I'll be there. Promise." He was so tired he could hardly put the phone back in its cradle.

"You know," he says, looking at my bald spot, "you should put a little sun block on that. You're beginning to glow." Last night I sat up listening to my CD of a 1951 performance at the Manhattan Center of *Carmen,* with Rise Stevens and Robert Merrill and Jan Pearce. I went right to the last act, thinking of Carmen running away with the matador Escamillo. Then Corporal Don Jose, who loves her, finds her. And he ends it all. I could see myself there, declaring my love even as I dispatch her, the music swelling. This opera that was such an initial flop, that became such a classic. Then I put on my CD of *La Traviata*, with Maria Callas singing in Mexico City, I listened to the deathbed duet of Alfredo and Violetta, the courtesan who agreed to give him up when his father said she would ruin his son. And I thought of my father telling me to go find Ziva in a hurry. Each father trying to save his son from... passion? Jealousy? Stupidity? My son Mark had called the night before to tell me he was going to marry his actress girlfriend Celeste in Vancouver, and he wanted me and Ziva there. "But your mother was just there," I said. "Dad, it's not the same. Besides, Celeste and I just decided this." I could imagine him with the fine dark hair he inherited from his mother, almost the same smile, the way it creases each side of his mouth, his eyes like mine, slow and steady in its gaze, appreciating a form, a color, a voice, a surface gleaming like the crystal fish sculpture we kept for years on the table under the hall mirror. He moves quickly, like his mother, an impatience coded into him, an awareness that inspiration is ephemeral, that human connectedness is no more durable than the yellow daylily's bloom. No wonder he wants to make films. To capture the nuance of desire in the shadows of objects, the half-light of a face, the frown, the clenched hand, the lilt of a word caught in flight. "We won't be able to put you up," he said. "That's okay. We'll stay at the Hotel Vancouver. I love that place." It's where Ziva and I spent two nights of delirious love-making, when we came out to see Mark in his new city, his new life. Before my mother died.

"Hey," my father says. "Sit up straight. Stop moping?" "I can't mope, if I'm sitting," I say. "For that I need to be standing." "Baloney," he says. "You I bet can mope even in dreams. You should be happy." He runs the clippers up the back of my neck. He turns away and coughs. "Aggh!" He blows his nose. "Excuse me," he says. "Did you take the Claritin?" I ask, knowing that it used to dry up his sinuses during allergy season. "Yes, I took the damn thing," he says. "Lean forward." He finishes with the clippers. Now he's combing what hair I have on top, patting it down. "Not so bad," he says. "You're not bald yet." "Great," I say. "What do I have, three weeks?" "Your health is all that matters," he says. "You worried you won't attract the girls?" "There's only one girl I worry about."

And like magic, there it is. A black Lincoln Town Car is pulling into the driveway. There are still some fallen catalpa leaves rimming the lawn like pieces of brown parchment. The leaves of the blown peonies each side of the driveway are black spotted, those huge blooms that each spring Ziva liked to bury her face in, the hot pinks, the golden-centered white ones, the rich deep scarlet ones, such soft-skinned beings she made me sniff and rub my nose in until I thought I had melded with another species. The frost-bitten hydrangea has crumpled just beneath my father's window — dark, wet, limp — and I am standing up, hair shedding off the towel, onto my father's carpet, and he's saying, "Hey, Harvey..." I see the back door of the Town Car open and out comes a long leg in jeans, then another. I think my heart is going to burst.

quale [kwa-lay]: *Eng.* n 1. A property (such as hardness) considered apart from things that have that property. 2. A property that is experienced as distinct from any source it may have in a physical object. *Ital.* pron.a. 1. Which, what. 2. Who. 3. Some. 4. As, just as.